AMISH RULE THE WORLD

A Martinus Publishing Anthology
Edited by Martin T. Ingham

Cover Art by Fruzsina Kovács

First Edition Released March 2022

Table of Contents:

The Shunning
By Diane Arrelle

My heart feels like it will explode. My mouth is so dry, but I finished my last bottled water half an hour ago. I have to urinate but to do so is just too undignified. Then again, I own the whole damned building, so I start to turn to the wall but—knowing everything here *is* mine—I turn to face the stairs leading down instead and release. Too bad the alien bastards weren't standing below me. I would have enjoyed christening them with my golden holy water.

The idea cheers me up, and so little cheers me up anymore. I am poor now instead of a financial leader of the whole damned continent. At least I am back in my own skyscraper, the largest building in a world that actually counts.

I stand and stare at the fire door up ahead. It has eighty-one written on it and I know that there are another ninety-four flights of stairs ahead of me. I guess the fact that I had paid the farm kids with chocolate bars and beer so they'd sweep the barn every night and plow the field every morning for me probably hadn't been the best idea. Perhaps, if I'd worked out a little bit, I wouldn't feel quite so out of shape now. Or perhaps, if I hadn't insisted on my tower being the tallest in the Americas, I wouldn't feel quite so overwhelmed climbing to my penthouse.

I sit down on the stairs to catch my breath and try to think. I think about that weird news report two years ago that signaled the end of life as I knew it. I remember how all the Amish and Mennonite people in this

1

country, as well as the other scattered, looney, tree hugging socialistic societies throughout the planet, vanished overnight. At least it may have been overnight, but then again who the hell paid any attention to them anyway with their stupid horse and buggies and their always keeping to themselves. They acted like they were better than the rest of the real Americans who worked to keep this country on the top of the heap.

Anyway, they were gone, just like the polar ice caps and the honeybees and nobody cared about any of that stuff anyway. Me, I spent all that time continuing to make money. I had this tower completed like a monument, tallest building of all time—that was until some Arab multi-billionaire beat my record. I decided right then and there to think of another way to be on top and decided to build luxury space resorts instead. It would have been so grand to have my international brand go interstellar, to be the most famous name in the cosmos.

I take a deep breath and shake off the frustrating memory. I have to get to the top before my last flashlight dies or I'll be plunged into eternal darkness. Maybe I should have put windows in the stairwells, but it doesn't matter. I am not going to die on the steps, to rot until my bones turn to dust. I am going home, to the top floor, to live in my penthouse, and the Amish life be damned.

I struggle and take step after step. My fourth flashlight is starting to grow dim. I've climbed 100 flights of stairs and used more than half my supply of lights. I know I have rooms filled with batteries galore in my apartment, but at my current rate of climbing, I realize I won't make it. I stop and sit again and close my eyes. I am exhausted. I need sleep and then, when I wake, I'll be fresh enough to climb faster.

* * *

My mind drifts back eighteen months when the message flashed through every mode of communication. Everyone thought it was an elaborate false news scheme invented by some super hackers.

The first message was simple: *Unite your families or sacrifice ever seeing them again.*

No big deal. It was a stupid message and I was between wives anyway.

Sure, it was weird, and no one paid it any real heed. A week later the message came again adding: *In ten Earth days, travel as you know it will cease.* Again, no one important really gave it any thought, especially me.

That was until the day all the planes fell from the skies, the ships at sea lost all ability to navigate, all vehicles of every kind shut off, all power plants and all electricity stopped working, and all communication ceased to exist. Even the space station shut down, killing all the scientists inside and the satellites began losing their orbits. Over the next month, space debris spattered down, killing thousands of people.

Batteries, common household batteries, seemed to have slipped through the grid, so flashlights and lanterns worked—at least for the life of the battery. I had planned to make a fortune and cornered the market. Somewhere in New Jersey there is a warehouse chock full of my investment reaching their expiration dates because I had bought cheap knockoffs and had planned to sell them high.

One day, a few weeks later, the power grid came back on for five hours. Spaceships appeared over every city and messages were broadcast all over the planet. "People of Earth, after much consideration we have decided to allow you to continue existing. The decision was difficult and the fine people we took from you are being returned. They have convinced us that everyone on Earth can live a wholesome existence; respecting your planet, respecting each other, and returning this world to its healthy natural state. Thus, we are creating on each continent peaceful, communal societies. You, in the Americas are to travel to the nearest Amish commune and join it. We have placed them every three hundred miles and you will be transported to your new homes.

The world, which was already in pandemonium over the loss of power and communication, went completely berserk. But not in the way I expected. Everyone was herded by the aliens to a nearby community, and ninety percent of the dumb, loser, human sheep went willingly. They gladly gave up their modern clothes and their modern ideologies in exchange for guidance on how to live and work without any real conveniences.

I had not gone willingly. I wasn't dumb enough to listen to subhuman alien scum. I stayed in my penthouse for weeks until they came for me and forced me down one hundred seventy-five flights of stairs, then made me walk through the empty streets of Manhattan to a waiting wagon. They dumped me in Pennsylvania near a farm in Lancaster County. Can you imagine a less dignified fate?

* * *

My eyes suddenly open in the pitch darkness. I had been asleep, but I am awake again, the wagon trip a fading memory. I try to walk the stairs slowly at an even pace in the dark. My year on the farm has taught me to fear the dark a lot less than I used too, but this is total darkness and after a few minutes, I turn on a flashlight. I walk for what I think must be days but the flashlight is still on, so I know not that much time has passed. Finally, after using my next to last flashlight I see the number 170 on the fire door. Five more floors, I have almost made it.

I am exhausted again and I sit and think about my year in hell. Oh, the Amish had welcomed us, made everyone see how good life could be without the modern worries. Get up in the morning, slip into dull, baggy clothes with no zippers or buttons. The lifestyle did help some, the obese lost weight, no one smoked after all the cigarettes were used up, and there just wasn't very much alcohol to find. The young readily adapted to working the fields and tending the animals. At night, after the sun set, the candles would be lit until an early bedtime plunged us into darkness. Every morning we rose with the sun. And no one cared who I was or who I had been. No one cared that I should be leading them.

I'd learned that those who could, escaped. Most fled to the cities only to find the streets and buildings looted and unlivable. Some people returned to the farms, others, well, who knows what happened to them, but I'm sure that since they didn't return to the farm, they either were too dumb to survive or they had found a better way to exist.

* * *

I give up thinking about the farm and get up. I climb my last five floors. After opening the fire door, I see my penthouse entrance in the beam of the flashlight. I reach under the mat and my key is still there. I figured I might need a key someday, so I'd stuck it there when the aliens came and got me. I didn't think anyone was going to climb one hundred and seventy-five stories on the off chance they'd find a key hidden nearby.

I unlock my door and strip naked. The rooms are cold, and through the floor to ceiling windows I see the sky is darkening. I feel overwhelmed by the luxury of thick plush carpeting under my feet as I walk to my bedroom and dress in clothing that almost fits. Everything is loose, I too have lost weight, but I enjoy pulling up my zipper and buttoning the small buttons on my shirt. I feel like me for the first time in what feels like forever. I walk over to the bar and pour a drink of fine, aged whiskey, then I sit on my favorite chair until I get bored. I go back into my bedroom, put on my silk pajamas, and go to bed. I am tired and emotionally exhausted. I want to talk, but of course I am alone. I am afraid to use my flashlight, to call attention to the fact that I am here, so I sleep. I know I have plenty to eat and drink here and I figure I am set for a long stay.

* * *

I wake feeling frightened. I can feel them closing in. Then I realize that's not true, it's just the dregs of another nightmare. The room is so dark, but the sky I see through the wall of windows is beautiful.

So many stars.

Sure, I see stars like that out on the farm, but this was Manhattan, the city that never sleeps. Yet, there's not a drop of light that isn't natural, which to me is totally unnatural. There are tears on my cheeks and I realize that I am crying for the death of my world. For the first time I realize that my way of life might actually be over.

But wait, I'd been a world leader, a winner! I'd been a captain of finance and the best scam artist the world had ever known. I can't just give up and rest on my laurels.

I realize that being one of the richest men in the world is just a bunch of meaningless words now. My money is valueless. I have no worth. I shudder when I recall that I was shunned. Me! Shunned! The damned community elders found out I had bartered my watch and rings for chocolates and beer from the new black market on the farm. They learned I'd traded my goods to get out of doing farm work and menial labor that was beneath someone as important as I was. They made an example of me. They humiliated me and shunned me. Wherever I was, wherever I went, everyone turned their backs to me. No one would look at me. It was like I didn't exist. Me not existing?!? Absurd.

Only, I did exist. I had been a very important man. I know I am still very important to the elders because me and the people like me, the men who had controlled the money of the old world, are being forced to live and work alongside all those losers. We are expected to work the hardest to return our world to balance. My being shunned is just icing on the cake for those using me as an example.

Finally, one night I stole a horse and buggy and worked my way back home. It wasn't easy, but I did it. Now, as I sit in my comfortable leather chair, drinking brandy and listening to the sound of the wind blowing outside my towering monument, I wait. I wait, longing to hear a voice. I know they'll be here someday soon to take me back and I know I'll be shunned even more. I know eventually I'll be kicked off the farm to live outside the communal life for good, to die alone in my shame.

Only I'll be prepared. I know there are others like me. The shunned. The people who cannot adjust to the Amish ways. I know there will be lots of geniuses like me and scientists living like fish out of water. And I know that after my shunning goes on long enough, I'll be completely forgotten.

In fact, I'm counting on it. Then I'll gather my people to me and I will create the world all over again. A world of coal burning steam engines. A world where my scientists will create fleets of cars fueled by those farmers' cow shit.

Amish Rule the World

And in a hundred years, when those aliens come back to check on us, they'll find that I own their new world. A world in my image!

~END~

The Eye of God
By T.L. Barrett

"And He said, 'Take now your son, your only son, whom you love, Isaac, and go to the land of Moriah; and offer him there as a burnt offering on one of the mountains of which I will tell you.'"

Genesis 22:2

1

When Amos Zook was seventeen and still practically wet from his baptism, he fell from the top of a high gable during a barn raising. This was a year before he married Eva Miller, and two years before losing her during the birth of their twins, Miriam and Gabriel.

The clear sky and his lofty perch afforded Amos a view that had stilled him to awe with its grandeur. The sawing and hammering below him faded as he took in the plots of spring green pastures below the high heath upon which the barn stood. He turned his head and his eyes caught sight of Mount Providence, which rose like a juggernaut over the entire county. An age ago, the faithful had erected an enormous eye of god on its peak.

When he had been but a boy, Amos had asked his father, Conrad, what materials had been used to construct such a marvel.

"Materials that could have gone into plows, nails, and more," Conrad said with a little sneer. "Put it out of your mind son, it is never wise to draw judgment down upon oneself."

Perhaps it was the beauty of the scene, or the hopeful feeling with which Amos had greeted the day, but he forgot his father's warning. As his eyes took in the eye, there was a flash that startled him. The hairs on the back of his neck stood on end. He felt an uncanny presence observing him. He suddenly felt naked up there. The eye pulled at him, as if to carry him closer for observation. For a moment it lifted him from his body, and he was carried through the air like a leaf on the wind. He tried to yell, but he had no mouth from which to yell. He looked back and saw his own body slumped at his perch, his eyes lidded heavily.

Terror assailed him, and he pushed against it. For a moment he drifted closer to his body, but then snapped in the air, like a fish barbed on a hook.

Please, God! His mind screamed. *Do not take me! I am young! I promise to give you children and raise them to your service if you do not take me!*

As if in answer, Amos felt a sudden release. His spirit flew back into his body with such a force that Amos stood before he could orient himself. The world swayed around him. His foot staggered back to find purchase against vertigo; instead, it found empty air.

He fell three stories and landed amongst his neighbors on his back with a sickening thud. Old man Wittmer was the closest, having just poured a glass of lemonade for himself from the pitcher that one of the womenfolk had left for the men. He saw the terrible truth and got down on his knees and prayed for the dead young man's soul. A few of Amos's peers hurried forward to help their friend, but saw well enough, and followed their elder to their knees.

They weren't even finished with the Lord's Prayer when Amos grunted and sat up, brought his hands up and felt all around himself. 'A miracle!' the men whispered to each other in hushed tones, as Amos slowly got to his feet and looked around.

Later, as Amos sat down and sipped Lemonade from a glass held by a trembling hand, Jacob Hilty, a rotund man who perpetually sweated, even in winter, asked him if he had felt the hand of God as it held him.

9

Amos had felt the dizzy rush of air, the sudden painful jarring impact and the air leaving him.

"I felt... something," he said.

"Well, my boy, I saw it. I saw the hand of God hold you and protect you! A miracle!" Jacob Hilty said.

2.

Within the next week, all manner of folks would stop by his father's house, and ask to see the young man who had been held in the hand of God. These visits were uncomfortable for Amos, for the most part. He did not know what to say to them, or what to say when they asked to touch him. Apparently, Jacob Hilty had told everyone in five counties of the miracle.

Young Eva Miller did not ask to touch him, but she touched his heart with her gentle curiosity. Amos remembered his promise to the Eye of God, and asked to see her again. She agreed.

When a group of wagons filled the barnyard bearing all manner of diseased and dying folk looking for deliverance, Conrad stopped his son from greeting them, went out and scolded the lot of them fiercely for their idolatry toward his son. After they had cleared out, Conrad went inside and gripped the back of his high back chair and looked down at his son.

"We must always tread carefully in this world, Amos," Conrad said. "We must never be proud of the gifts with which God has graced us. We must never reveal..." he shifted, opened his mouth and then closed it again. "We must never test God's love in front of others." Father and son stared at each other for a long time. Amos apologized and promised that he would stay upright and humble before God.

"There will be a meeting of the Zooks," Conrad pronounced like a prophet.

3

Sure enough, the Zooks started to arrive the next day. Amos, pleased to be in the company of cousins and kin that he rarely saw, almost forgot that he was of age now, and would be expected to attend the gathering in his father's house rather than play with the other young folk as he had been wont to do.

It was a strange thing to pass Auntie Rebecca playing a mouth harp on the porch, with Uncle Eli, eyes closed and humming discordantly beside her, as they always did, instead of joining the other grown-ups. For a long moment, Amos tarried, being carried away by the strange melody that his relatives produced. He forgot everything and stood there slack until his father came out, grabbed him by the arm and pulled him inside.

The Zook elders were an odd and canny bunch. There was something formidable about their open-eyed stares that told that they saw more than they would ever speak. After they led Amos to a chair in the center of the room, Great Uncle Aaron came forward and wrapped his arms around the back of Amos. The embrace felt oddly comforting to Amos. Aaron's long white beard felt soft against the back of his neck; Amos felt only love and protection from his great Uncle.

Then Aaron leaned forward and began to whisper whirling words into Amos's ear. As the old patriarch did so, Amos's eyes grew wider and wider.

"We are not what we seem," the whispers told him. "Long ago, when the people had come to understand the Lord, our father, they lived high in the mountains of Switzerland. God then made a distinction between his faithful children who lived in the valleys, the Emmantaler, and those who lived in the mountains, the Oberlanders. God tasked the Oberlanders to spread the truth to the world and save mankind from sin and the fruits of their own proud machinations. To do so he gave them gifts that were not of this world. It was forbidden to the Oberlanders to mix their seed with the other races of mankind.

"A prophetess named Deborah then walked among the Oberlanders. She said that her spirit had travelled deep inside of Mount Jungfrau and there had seen hidden lost holy books. She told her followers that a savior would be born, that would raise the Oberlanders to the heavens, the liberator, the second coming of the most holy.

"When the Oberlander elders heard that a woman had claimed a messiah would be born, but of mixed blood, an abomination in the sight of God, on some unsanctified earth far away, they ordered the prophet to be locked away and all who spread her prophecies to be so punished. Deborah had foreseen this and gathered her people to her. They used their gifts to escape. They crossed the western waters and lived among the people in secret. Ten tribes, of which Zook was but one, left with the prophetess. They must hide their gifts and lay no claim to their mountain birthright. Someday they will return to the mountain; their messiah will see it done. They will open the forgotten books and all will be as is promised in scripture.

"Until then, we are known only as the Prodigal, the secret outcast. We know each other for there are 10 prodigal tribes, and X will be the sign with which we will know each other."

All of the Zook family members present solemnly crossed their forearms in front of their chests.

It took a while for Amos to realize that the elders had once again taken up their council with each other while he sat in their center looking dazed and foolish. His mind so whirled with placing this new truth beside all he had known and experienced that even when he did hear their words, he marked few of them.

"Should the council of Deborah be sought out?" Aunt Leah asked.

"No, not for this, surely!" Conrad growled.

"Something must be done about this Jacob Hilty!" Cousin James said.

"I will take care of it," Conrad said.

4.

Conrad invited Jacob Hilty to his house. Hilty came because Conrad did not extend many invitations and no one ever refused Conrad anything. Ity angered Conrad when Hilty refused to be silenced when it came to what he had witnessed around Amos.

"Your behavior is not reverent, nor humble," Conrad said.

"Are we not told by scripture to bear witness to the glory of God?" Hilty retorted.

"Keep your tongue, and keep yourself from flattering company or may your head split like a bear-ravaged honeycomb!" Conrad pronounced. Hilty hitched where he sat in the parlor. His eyes glazed. Slowly he raised a trembling hand up to his head as if feeling for a wound.

"I feel so strange. If you will excuse me!" He staggered when he tried to rise. Conrad caught and steadied him.

"You do not realize how circumspect you are toward the wonders of God's miracles," Hilty said, then groaned and clutched at his head. Conrad helped his guest back into his cart and returned to his house. When he did, he gave his son a queer apprehensive look and said, "Guard yourself."

Amos did just that. A second-hand paranoia crept into his routine, a constant anxious thrum of concern and alertness. This was due to that queer look of apprehension that his father had given him. Amos had only seen its like once, when he was quite young and after Conrad had read to him from the book of Genesis, and Amos had asked, "If God told you to kill me, like he told Abraham to sacrifice Isaac, would you do it?"

His father had merely shone that apprehensive look down upon his son and said, "Yes, if God should ask it of me," he said.

"But, how would you know if it is God?" Amos asked.

"Because I will know, just like you must know when you have children of your own," Conrad said.

Amos thought about this for a long moment.

"No, I would never be as cruel as you! I would never kill my children!"

In response, Amos enforced a strict time of fasting for his son and hard heavy labor so that he would think twice before questioning scripture and his father's character. If Conrad seemed cruel to his son, it must be noted that never at any time did he use the powerful tongue God had given him on his son, nor any member of his family.

5

Five years after the death of Amos's beloved wife, and just one year from when one of the Grabers' in-bred and ill-natured work horses stomped quiet Conrad Zook's incredibly gifted tongue once and for all, Amos began to understand the anxiety his father had felt when he was young.

When the eldest Graber boy came bursting into his yard yammering for aid and assistance with the killers of Amos's father, Amos looked up toward the dripping April sky, sighed, and shook his head. *Why does it always feel like God is testing me?* he thought to himself. He would do the neighborly thing, for the Eye of God hung everywhere, and of course, Amos was that kind of man.

However, Amos's children did not make the wet and dangerous chore any easier as they mooned and grew respectfully teary-eyed when he told them that he would not be able to read to them nor take them outside to play as was their wont to do on Saturday Afternoons.

Esther, Amos's younger sister who helped with the children and the house, called Gabriel, Amos's shadow. That had been part of the reason Amos had decided on building furniture and wood sculpting. It allowed his son to stay in sight and learn a trade. It didn't hurt that the trade was lucrative, and Amos was a natural. The wood seemed to carve like butter under his steady hands. He could drive a nail plumb in in one smack, a strategy that he couldn't seem to teach to anybody else. Although, no one tried harder than Gabriel did.

"Can I pleath come with you?" Gabriel said through a spring head cold. Amos ruffled his son's curly locks and smiled.

"I love it that you want to, my son, but you are not well," Amos said. "But I saw your Aunt Esther with an armful of books she brought down from the attic!"

"Father, don't forget to check the belly strap on Blondie's saddle," Miriam said, appearing out of nowhere as she was wont to do. Amos squinted his eyes.

"What did you say?" he asked, smiling despite himself.

"The strap that goes on the belly…" Miriam said, swinging her arms wide and gesticulating for clarity.

"The girth?"

"Yeah, that's it! Check it! And, father, walk to the horse on the side, not up the hill or down the hill, to the horse…the gray horse with white spots." Miriam said.

"Wow, that's pretty specific!" Amos said enjoying this miniature version of the same routines he had once only too briefly endured with her mother. "Is there anything else I should be aware of?"

"Oh, oh, oh, tell Mrs. Graber that her bread is going to burn," she said.

"Well, now that just seems pretty rude to say to someone—" Amos started.

"No, if you don't say anything, her bread will burn. That will be rude, so say it as soon as you see her! Promise!" She said emphatically.

"All right, I promise," Amos said and held up his hands in surrender. She hugged his leg.

"Oh, and ask them for a slice for each of us!" She added.

"Pleath!" Gabriel added for both of them.

"Let your father go, so he can get back, children!" Esther admonished as she entered the room, book in hand. Amos kissed both heads before thanking his sister and hurrying out into the rain before he could change his mind.

6

Amos found Mrs. Graber in the barnyard greeting other neighbors that had come to help. Some of the men looked surprised to see him, and were overtly gregarious toward him after the awkward silence as those gathered remembered last year's loss. Mrs. Graber thanked him profusely for coming and informed the men that her husband, Ike, was up in the high pasture already. When the men turned to find Ike, Amos paused.

"Mrs. Graber, do I smell bread burning?" he asked. Men paused to sniff at the air, but shook their heads. Mrs. Graber put a hand to her head.

"Oh, dear! In the commotion, I almost forgot!" she said and scurried toward her porch. Before she got there, she sniffed and turned.

"God has blessed you with a strong sense of smell, Amos Zook," she said and went inside.

"I didn't smell anything," Albrecht King said beside Amos.

Amos shrugged and led the men toward the high pasture.

When Amos came around the Graber's stables after proudly returning the first of Graber's itinerant horses (and without totally spoiling his clothes), he caught movement out of the corner of his eye. He turned, and there was Gabriel in his white nightwear standing in the dripping rain. For just a moment, Gabriel's eyes met Amos's and grew very wide.

Then he was gone. Amos called to him. After the third call, Albrecht King answered and came running over the grassy mound of pasture that rose up over the farm's outbuildings.

"Are you all right, Amos?" he managed through panting. Amos could see the lines of worry on Albrecht's face. The man had witnessed the death of Amos's father the year before; Amos felt suddenly guilty for alarming him. Amos looked about himself one more time and nodded his head.

"We've cornered the big one in the pasture. If you can come, maybe we can keep it from breaking through the fence," Albrecht said, a hand pressed to his chest as if to calm his pounding heart.

When the two got to the high pasture, the workhorse, gray with dappled white spots, was putting on a show of prancing and preparing for battle on the steep bank. A few men with poles had skirted above and were just outside the fence, trying to deter the horse from making a break for freedom. Below the horse, on a slope that descended to a little tarn of manure and spring rain, sidled four fellows ascending slowly in an attempt to box in the horse. Amos could see the folly in this almost immediately. In a quiet voice he told Albrecht to return to the stable and swing the doors wide open. Albrecht nodded and gingerly made his way down the slick bank. Amos noticed that the rain had stopped, leaving a delicate stillness to the scene.

Slowly, Amos climbed a little higher, then turned and walked toward the Horse on a level with it. He spread his arm and began talking softly as if to a small child. When the horse saw him, it wheeled about, nearly floundered and reared up. The men below startled. They slipped and slid on the grass as they realized their precarious position below the horse. Only Ike Graber remained, turning his head to see his companions retreat, and then watching as Amos approached the gray stallion.

For a moment, Amos was certain that he had managed to calm the horse, and would be able to walk up and grab the horse's head collar. Then, Ike called up to warn Amos to be careful. The horse wheeled and began a wild descent straight down the bank. Below them, Ike paled, turned and dashed down the slick bank. Amos watched the two descend, surely the crazed animal would trample its master, but then just at the base, Ike turned and leapt clear of the horse's path. He almost cleared the manure pond that had formed there, but landed waist deep on the far end instead. The horse slowed as it mounted the next crest, then trotted down and went directly into the stable. Albrecht quickly shut and barred the door behind it.

A cheer went up from the men above, but then they turned and saw Ike trying to wade gingerly through the filth in which he had jumped. All of the men converged there, as Ike's relatives, wet from their falls upon the bank, helped him up and out of the muck.

Everyone was quiet as he looked down at himself. His relatives and neighbors, many having grown with the man from childhood, knew and feared his fits of temper.

Instead, when Ike looked back up, however, his speckled face broke into a cheery grin, and he began to sing. It was: "God Be with You Till We Meet Again", and his tenor sounded clear in the little dell formed by the sloping banks. Soon all the men joined in, and Amos, too, singing deeply, their heads raised toward the blue April sky. Sweet echoes reverberated over the valley; the Graber women folk gathered on their porch to listen at first, and then raised their own voices to contribute to the euphony.

*

When Amos returned his sister gave him a rare and unrestrained hug. When her brother had gone to attend to a chore that had killed their father the year before, it must have driven her mad with worry. Their mother had died from the measles when they were young, and while most nuclear families in the county boasted anywhere from five to twelve children, Amos was Esther's sole sibling. Once, Grandmother King had said that Amos and his sister had been God's blessing to soothe the ache of her mother losing five babies before him. It was much the same with the other Zooks, and Amos had attributed it to the secret Oberlander blood in them.

"Gabriel, how is he? Have you checked on him?" Amos asked his sister, his mind going to the boy's strange appearance and disappearance near Graber's stable.

"Yes, he fell asleep before I had chance to read a paragraph," Esther told him. Miriam and I have been quilting downstairs, but we just checked in on him a little less than an hour ago. He was singing in his sleep. I've never heard such a thing!"

"Singing in his sleep," Amos said and cocked an eyebrow. "What was my son singing in his sleep?"

"God Be with You Till We Meet Again," she said.
"Father!" Gabriel said from the doorway. His eyes were puffy from sleep as he stood in his white night wear. He came forward and reached his arms up to be lifted. Amos complied.

"Aunt Esther said that you were singing," Amos said.

"I was singing, you were singing, Mister King was singing! Everyone was singing!" Gabriel said. "But Mr. Graber was the first to sing." His features screwed up as if dutifully stifling hilarity: "And he had fallen in the poop, right up to his waist!" he said.

"How do you know this, child," Amos asked the boy.

"I was there! You saw me!" he protested.

"No, Amos, the boy speaks false. He did not leave his bed until just now," Esther said.

"To speak the truth," Amos said. "I thought I did spy you near the stable, but nobody else saw you."

"Nobody has ever seen me when I walk in my sleep, just you, father," the boy said and squeezed his father's neck and kissed his cheek. Esther and Amos shared a look of worry. Amos gently placed the boy seated on the kitchen tabletop, whose eyes grew wide at this forbidden position.

"Have you ever walked in your sleep before?" Amos asked.

"Yes, plenty of times," Gabriel said. "Was it wrong? Was it a sin?" His aspect grew somber and his eyes lowered.

"No," Amos said, and brushed the boy's locks with his fingers. "God has given you a gift, but it is a secret gift. You should never boast of it, for that is proud, and never tell others that you have it, for God did not give such a gift to others. No one has ever seen you before this, are you certain?"

Gabriel nodded. "You are the only one."

"You must be very careful no one ever does. Only use your gift when you know God wants you to, or to keep your sister safe always, that is your job, all right?"

"And what is my job?" Miriam asked from behind them.

"Well, little one," Esther said. "You must look after Gabriel, and make sure he is safe."

"But, I cannot walk in my sleep!" Miriam said plaintively. "Why didn't I get the gift, too?"

Esther looked to Amos, who shrugged.

"Hey, guess what Mrs. Graber gave us?" Amos said, and proffered a half loaf of brown bread from his coat pocket. Both children's eyes widened as if they meant to beat their mouths to the feast. Amos pulled the bread back for a moment.

"Miriam, how did you know that Mrs. Graber was baking bread?" Amos asked.

Miriam shrugged. "Mrs. Graber bakes the best bread," she said.

"I thought you said you liked my baking best," Esther said.

"Biscuits," Gabriel said. "Your biscuits are the best!"

Before Amos had shooed the children off to play they had convinced their aunt to bake a batch of biscuits. Amos sat at the table, lost in thought about what all of this meant.

7

Nine months before Esther wed David Yoder and five years before the Ascension, Esther woke Amos from deep sleep. He awoke confused from a dream about the Widow Lapp, who had been increasingly present in their lives, and it took a moment before he could hear his daughter's voice coming from her bed chamber. This was just before the twins' seventh birthday.

They found Miriam asleep in her bed, her open eyes showing only white, strange garbled words spilling from her mouth. As Esther went to fetch a lantern, Amos stood with his skin all gooseflesh as his daughter hissed these strange syllables.

"Miriam?" he called softly. His daughter fell silent.

"Father?" she said in a faraway voice. Esther brought the lantern, the light of which revealed that the girl was still in a deep trance.

"Miriam, where are you?" he asked.

"The Ascension," she said. Aunt and father looked at each other in astonishment.

"What do you see?" Esther asked.

"Our people are rising to the heavens, like stars." Her slack face curved into a great grin, and a sob escaped her lips. Tears spilled from her fluttering eyes.

"I am the liberator. It shall be accomplished." A desperate fear chilled Amos's heart. He reached forward and touched the side of the girl's face.

"Miriam, wake up," he said. Her hand shot up and grasped his forearm.

"Simon and Solomon will take us across the ocean!" she said around an impossible background of hissing and garbled sounds. Both Amos

20

and Esther looked up to the shelf where Miriam kept the two odd dolls of little men she had made the summer before. Amos relaxed with a slow grin.

"They will? Who else is there? Is Horse-horse there with us?" Amos asked, referring to his son's favorite toy.

"Do not jest!" the little girl said in a husky and throaty rasp. "All depends on you."

Amos went to rouse his daughter, desperate to get her to stop making the uncanny sounds. Esther caught his arm.

"Am I there with you?" Esther asked the sleeping girl.

"No, you are with your children in your new house with your new husband," Miriam said.

"Well, then what about the Widow Lapp?" Esther said and wrinkled her nose up at her brother.

"No, the widow Lapp will die in one year and three days," Miriam said.

"That's enough," Amos said and shook her. "Wake up, child!"

For a moment, she did. Her eyes came open, looked at her father, reached up, hugged his neck, drawing him to stoop over the bed. When she released him, she fell back to the bed, deep in slumber.

Downstairs, later, Esther paced about the kitchen, while Amos sat in his thinking chair and thought.

"Your daughter is a prophet," Esther said.

"We don't know that," Amos said.

"We do know that. You know that," Esther said. "She said she was the Liberator! I didn't even know the children knew such words." Could his daughter possibly be the second coming?

"I cannot believe this? I will not believe this," Amos said.

"I didn't know we had a choice," Esther said.

"I cannot stand by and watch my child suffer. I do not hope to have the grace of the Virgin Mother!" he hissed and pounded a fist against the table. "I will not lose her!"

"You will never lose me!" Miriam said from behind them. Her eyes still fluttered open to reveal only whites. "Do not doubt your destiny! You shall be at my side for the Ascension!"

Amos carried the child back to bed, and when he returned he swore his sister to secrecy.

One year and three days later, the Widow Lapp, died of a raging fever that took her in the dark of night.

8.

Five years later, when his children were twelve, Amos was about to break the third commandment and finish a chest of drawers after service when Gabriel found his father in his workshop.

"Father, you must do something!" Gabriel said. His face was ashen, and he trembled as he came into the workshop. Seeing his son's face set so, Amos dropped his hammer and ran to him.

"What is it? What has happened?" Amos asked. It took a few minutes for Amos to get the full story out of his son. It alarmed him to hear Jacob Hilty's name come from his son's mouth. Amos had not thought of the man in a long time. Once Jacob Hilty had been a gregarious busy-body, but in the past fourteen years, Jacob had retreated from society. When he was seen, which was not often, it was with a cloth wrapped tight around his head, as if to ward off a toothache. Practically every Sunday one of his family or neighbors would ask for prayers for the man who was terribly afflicted.

For years, Gabriel and Jacob Hilty's daughter, Grace, had developed a close bond of friendship as children are wont to do when their elders are occupied by society. When Gabriel had expressed dismay about how tentative Grace had grown of late, his sister said that it was normal for girls to grow so modest as they become women. However, on this Sunday, Gabriel had seen the tears in her eyes and watched how his old friend trembled and ducked her head whenever someone raised a voice. He had tried desperately to get her alone, to find out what was bothering Grace, but the girl shied away from these attempts with a sad shake of her head and a turning away.

When they had gotten home, Gabriel had sat down and walked in his sleep to Jacob Hilty's.

"He's planning on killing all of them! He's already killed Grace's brother! Father he is going to feed them to the pigs!" he said, tears cascading down his face. Amos crushed his trembling son against his chest and rubbed his head.

"He's telling the truth," Miriam said, suddenly appearing at their side and startling Amos.. "You will save some of them, if you hurry!" she said.

Amos sat his son down and walked out into the barnyard. He looked to the stable, then looked down the road. A feeling of desperate urgency overtook him. He broke into a run, like he had only run in secret between far hills as a young man, reveling in the gifts God had given him, racing to beat the wind. Bends, bridges and farms flashed by. Then, before he knew it, he was standing just outside Jacob Hilty's barn.

Voices wept and wailed from within. Amos crept to the door and pulled it slowly open. He stepped forward and blinked to see in the muted light of the barn's interior. What he saw made him wish he had not. What looked like the entire Hilty family dangled over a pig sty from chains wrapped around a frame beam. Sure enough, Hilty's eldest, Caleb, hung slack, his stomach torn open, and his bowels spilling out into the sty, where the greedy pigs tugged at it.

Jacob Hilty, further back in the barn, and Amos saw each other at the same moment. Hilty's face was barely visible beneath the swaddling of cloth wrapped tightly about the man's head.

"Conrad Zook!" The man shouted. "You have done this to me, and set bees buzzing in my head!" He grabbed a scythe off the wall, and tramped forward. "I will send you to your eternal reward for it!"

Amos stepped back, trying to make sense of the scene, speechless in his shock and panic. Jacob Hilty advanced. Amos put a hand out, and the mad murderer swung his scythe.

Amos's fingers on his left hand flew through the air and landed across the barn floor before him. Both of the men looked down at them for a moment. When Hilty looked up a wide porcine grin covered his face and he snorted glee. A scruffy dog shot out from the shadows and grabbed up one of the fingers in its mouth.

Something broke inside of Amos. He growled, and the look of rage that crossed his features made the laughing maniac pause. In what seemed one movement, Amos strode forward, kicked the mongrel across the barn and grabbed Hilty by his fat neck. The scythe fell to the barn floor. Hilty gasped. Amos could feel the fiend's throat give with a crunch as he squeezed. Hilty's eyes grew comically huge, as Amos lifted the man one handed and hurled him into the far wall of the barn. There was a crack and a wet sound as both the barn boards and the murderer's skull broke.

When Amos went to help the strung-up would-be victims, they squealed and shirked away from him. He growled at them, and when that would not still them, he roared. He managed, with his one unwounded hand, to get a boy free. When Amos set him down, the boy scooted away from him in a panic.

"Mrs. Hilty!" he managed after backing away from the sight of pigs feasting on human entrails. "Have your son free you." He stepped on one of his own fingers as he backed away. "God has saved you," he said quickly, and then left the awful place.

When Amos got home, he went to his bedroom and lay down. His hand throbbed bolts of pain up his arm and then through his chest, making him bite down so hard he thought he might crack his own teeth. He was amazed to see, however, that the bleeding that had occurred immediately upon receiving the grievous wound had stopped. The angled stubs on his savaged hand had already begun scabbing over.

When he put his head back, he fell into a blissful slumber.

*

His children brought food and drink to his bed. He had a vague memory of eating savagely, grasping at the meat they gave him and choking them down, bones and all. He fought to keep his eyes open.

Once, when his mind whirled in the agony of his bones knitting themselves back into being, he looked to the doorway and saw his

24

daughter standing there, her eyes fluttering and white.

"The ascension comes! All will depend on you!" she said and then joined the litany of flashing grotesque images that assailed his dreams.

9

Three days later, Amos held his savaged hand up to the light of the window and studied it. His fingers had grown back. The skin there had just started to grow back in patches like scales under a slimy, almost embryonic goo.

"Amos," a familiar man's voice came from the doorway. "We need to talk."

Amos turned to see his cousin, Baker Zook, standing in the doorway and itching one of his enormous ears with his fingers.

"A meeting has been called?" Amos asked with a grunt.

"No," Baker said. "It has gone beyond that. The others will not come."

"Why?" Amos asked.

"People are talking. I am very good at hearing things, remember?" Baker said, gesturing to the huge flaps of skin and cartilage on either side of his head. "At least three people witnessed you running faster than a race horse across half the county. You showed up to a farm you have not visited in at least twenty years, just in time to save most of the Hilty family. There you killed Jacob Hilty one handed, by throwing him through the barn wall. People are talking. They even kept your fingers as evidence.

"They will shun us, then?" Amos asked.

"Would you expect anything else?" Baker retorted.

"No, but my children!" Amos said. "They are still so—"

"You and your children have put every Prodigal in the new world in mortal danger. The Oberland authorities have been called," Baker said.

"Who would do such a thing?" Amos asked.

"Jeremiah Lapp," Baker said, the brother of the deceased Widow Lapp. The man had been cold and rude ever since the passing of his late sister. Amos had guessed that the man blamed him somehow for his

25

sister's death, or at the least, for letting the woman die alone.

"Where should I go? How will we live?" Amos asked.

"You must go to the Deborah-in-the-hills," Baker said, and a cold chill pierced Amos.

After Baker had gotten down with Amos on his knees and prayed for deliverance, he hugged his cousin once and turned his back, forever more. Amos, tears coursing his cheeks, watched Baker board his cart and leave.

Eventually, he wiped away the tears, packed some clothes in a bag, and went to find his children. He found his son, slumped over, seemingly asleep, in the corner of the parlor. Gabriel would not awaken.

"What is wrong with your brother?" Amos asked when he found his daughter packing supplies into their wagon in the yard.

"What do you mean?" she asked.

"He is asleep in the parlor. He will not wake!" Amos said. She scurried to the parlor and fretted over her brother. When she failed to rouse him, her shoulders sank.

"What did you do?" Amos asked. He felt that strange prickling heat, so intoxicating and so new, under his skin.

"He asked me what would happen, and I told him that it was time for the Ascension. I told him that we will travel to the Oberland, and the world will know the secrets inside Jungfrau Mountain. He said that he would fly in his sleep over the ocean and see what was waiting there."

"And you let him?" Amos asked. His daughter stepped back from him. "What if he gets lost, and can't find his way back? What if—" He stopped, stooped, and shook his son.

"Wake up, Gabriel!" Amos shouted.

"He will not wake today, father!" Amos looked up at his daughter, so sure in her foretelling, and a kind of sullen resentment filled him. He sneered.

"We must travel to the city of Boston, on the coast," she said.

"We will do no such thing," he said. "Finish packing the wagon. We are going to see the Deborah."

10

Cousin Baker's parting directions led Amos and his children to a desolate grotto deep in the hills. Gabriel slept in the back, and Miriam sat expectantly beside him, regarding their progress aloofly.

"Stay in the wagon. Mind your brother." Amos said. He picked his way over dead logs and through brambles. The grotto wound round a corner and then he climbed a slope to a little ridge that ran along the side of a steep hill.

When he saw the cave opening, and the little plume of smoke rising from it, every instinct in his body told him to turn and hurry back to his children. Instead, he fingered his regenerated fingers until the sensitive new skin burned with the contact. Taking a deep breath, he marshaled himself and approached.

"Come in, come in, grandchild!" a parchment dry voice slipped into his ear. Amos stooped and entered.

He half crawled for the first few feet and then the cave opened into a chamber. Pots of incense burned away. Bones, and skin lay discarded in piles to the side. Ahead of him, the chamber curved up to about chest level, where a second cavern began. Amos sensed movement there, and took a step back.

A dry chuckling sound came from that cobweb-festooned tunnel. This was followed by a shape scuttling forth. An ancient woman peered down at Amos from the lip of that tunnel. Her face was hidden behind some kind of mask that appeared to be carved from bone. Above this, sprouted a mass of cobwebs, dust, and dreads. Speechless, Amos studied the fearsome figure before him.

"Zook, Zook, Zook! You come looking for direction, yes?" she asked.

Amos nodded his head.

"You will have to speak up, my ears are older than the wind with which you draw breath," she said.

"Yes, are you the Deborah?" he asked. More of the unsettling chuckling sounds commenced.

"Yesssss!" the ancient behind bone said. "I have travelled across the great waters with my children, looking for the voice of God. I could not find it in the mountains of my birth. The people there followed the dictates of a terrible thing without a soul, a demi-urge!"

She let out a cry from the painful memory. It echoed around him, and through him.

"I came here, and waited for the prophecy, and listened for the voice of God. It took me a long time to learn the language of the wind, the tongue of the waters and the rain. I heard the song of the bird and the buzzing of the flies, and then I put them all together. In that quiet place inside me, I found it."

"It said, 'Deborah! You have been tricked. You have thought yourself free, but you have only followed the machinations of that terrible false-mind inside the mountain. Since then, I have tried to dream of the truth, to find some way to truly liberate this world from the madness of our people." She stopped and was so still, Amos thought her asleep.

"I dreamt last week, or three years ago!" she pronounced loudly. "I dreamt of another Earth, where men keep the Eye of God folded in their wallets. Shining towers rise and threaten the sky, and they are filled with the sins and degradations of man. Surely, I thought, these indolent wretches swarming over the planet are free! But, as I looked closer, I could see that here they were, still, our people, ancient and refusing to die, hidden in the pockets of the world. There they played with the desires of men's minds. There they gave out the lie of power, and mankind groveled not in prayer but in the sparkle of novelty and sin. No, there is no escape from it."

Although Amos did not understand what the ancient woman was saying, he understood the despair in her voice, and his last hope began to wither.

"Deborah, what must I do to protect my children and find a way to raise them in this world?" Amos asked.

"I have heard the Lord, God on high!" the ancient screamed. "I have heard his summons in a cricket song. Do you believe it?"

"Yes!" Amos said. "How can I wake my son?"

"You cannot. If he awoke, he would not be your son," she said.

"That cannot be! What am I to do?"

"You must kill your daughter. Sacrifice her to God. Save us all from what is to come!"

There was a long silence, as the words of Deborah struck home in Amos's heart.

"No," Amos said.

"What?" the Deborah roared.

"I will not slay my child. God surely does not want me to do so," he said.

"Fool!" She screamed. "You will cast us all to eternal servitude! No, I will not let you! If you will not kill the child, then I will!"

The woman began to move forward, her brittle looking head and arms rising over the lip of the tunnel entrance. Behind it, came a great length of shining scales. It flowed toward him. It cast its mask off, and the diamond eyes of a serpent bore into his.

"Do not ssstand in my way, grandchild!" the serpent hissed.

Feeling dazed, Amos stepped to the side. The long serpentine body of the creature slid toward the entrance of the cave.

"No," Amos whispered. "No!" he screamed and leapt. He wrapped his arms around the creature's torso and squeezed. The Deborah lurched, hissed and clawed. Amos squeezed with all of his strength. Amos's blood flowed from the wounds that the claws left. The serpent writhed against the walls, and the stone dug into Amos's back and arms, but still he squeezed.

Something deep in the creature cracked. The Deborah fell slack. Serpent and man lay like spent lovers on the floor of the cave.

Amos Zook returned to his children in the grotto at twilight. Although his wounds had already closed, they burned with venomous sting, and his head raged with heat. When Miriam saw her father, she paled and looked as if she might run. Amos remembered the terrible voice of the serpent woman and studied his peculiar daughter. She still did not speak, but watched him warily as he went by her. He crawled into the back of the wagon, gathered his sleeping son to his chest and slept.

Miriam clucked at the horse and steered them back toward the long road to Boston.

11

Only once before, when he was quite young, had Amos been to the coast. His father, seated beside him on the wagon, had warned his son: "The people of the sea are a different sort, live a different life. They sin to beat the devil on shore and then trust their lives to the fury of God's waves. They are all doomed to hell, and mad. Stay close, stay aware, and keep God in your heart." Amos had been amazed by the diseased and starving in the streets, many of them children. When a woman wearing very little on her body had approached the wagon, Conrad had slapped his son for gawking.

In all these years, the city of Boston had not changed. After the long days under his daughter's directions, letting her steer the horse, he forgot how young she really was. She began asking impertinent questions about the strange behavior of the smoking, drinking louts and their whores as they approached the docks.

Amos caught sight of two men, one short and wide, the other tall and thin, loitering under the eaves of a storefront. One of them stared fixedly at his daughter as they passed, and got his companion's attention, who did then as the first.

"Miriam, get in the back with your brother and stay there," Amos ordered.

"No," she said and turned to look at him with such defiance, Amos was tempted to slap her. His blood tingled with that fury once more. "I am the liberator, father. God will protect me!"

"Girl, you don't even know what those two men back there want to do to you. Listen and obey, or so help me, God-" Amos growled.

"What two men? Where? Where are they?" she said.

"Just back there, and if you're lucky and quiet and do as I—" he started.

"Turn around! It's them!" she reached for the reins. Amos growled and pulled them away from her. The horse, confused, gave a neigh of protest and balked at going further.

The two men were standing together beside the wagon. They both got down and bowed very low, so that their heads were almost touching the filth in the street. When they stood, the short, wide one raised his arms and crossed them over his chest. Amos studied them for a long moment, and then slowly crossed his own arms across his chest.

"Who are you? What do you want?" Amos asked them.

"I am Solomon," the smaller one said, "and this is Simon. We are here to provide passage for the Liberator."

*

They booked passage on a ship across the Atlantic under the pretense of being pilgrims on their way to the homeland. The ship steward looked like he was about to make a fuss over Gabriel, who he believed must be sick with some contagious plague. Simon walked away with him to discuss the matter, and came back alone a while later. No one else spoke to them for nearly the entire trip, and Amos did not see the steward again.

Amos spent most of the trip trying to pour gruel into his son's mouth and praying to God to deliver them safely to their destiny.

12

As Amos trembled and looked upon the great Eye of God that rose high above Jungfrau mountain, he wondered if this was how Moses had felt when he had approached the slopes of Mt. Sinai. He felt unworthy, filled with fear and doubt, naked before that terrible eye.

Would God restore his son? Could his daughter really be the chosen one who would liberate us from the earthly sin? Hope had brought him this far, across an ocean and half a continent to this place. He kneeled with his son in his arms and prayed. He whispered his faith, he felt his love.

The child stirred! The boy murmured, and his eyes flew open.

"My boy!" Amos said, tears clouding his vision. He pulled the boy close and held him tight. The boy began to struggle. Amos surprised, was caught off balance, and fell onto his back. Gabriel slithered out of his grasp and deftly picked himself up as if he hadn't spent nearly the last season in a slumber.

"Gabriel, do not be afraid," Amos said and reached for him. Gabriel stared coldly at his father, and then slunk between Simon and Solomon. He took their hands, and when they leaned down, Gabriel whispered in their ears. They nodded.

"It is time," Miriam said. Their two traveling companions nodded again.

"I don't understand," Amos said.

"First you must be purified," Miriam said.

Amos reached out to push himself up from where he had fallen, and his hand closed over a sharp rock.

A raven perched in a nearby tree called out: "Kill her! Kill her! Kill her!"

For a moment, Amos looked into the cold eyes of his children, and he tested the rock against his palm. The world seemed to hold its breath.

For a moment, he thought he would throw the rock at his own flesh and blood. For a moment, it looked as if Miriam expected him to throw it.

"Get up!" she ordered. Amos, sighed and rose. Miriam came and took his hand and led him toward the Mountain.

As they went, Amos remembered his daughter's prophecy:

"Do not doubt your destiny! You shall be at my side for the Ascension!"

*

They went inside the mountain, though it felt to Amos like the mountain had swallowed them. Strange smells and colorful lights surrounded them. A great presence filled the caverns through which they walked. That presence grew until it was a silent scream that filled

Amos's mind. Was this God? He wondered. Suddenly fear assailed him. He tried to shake his daughter's hand free. He tried to turn and run back the way they had come. Simon and Solomon gripped his arms. Their hands were cold and rough as they guided him onward into a great cavern inside the mountain.

Strange figures stood, prayed or slithered in the shadows. Ahead of them a great shining metallic pyramid filled the far end. Above the pyramid sat a great eye. In horror, Amos knew that it would open.

Amos cursed. Amos bit. Amos spit and flailed and wept. Simon and Solomon lifted him, and Amos's own children grabbed his legs and helped carry him out into the center of the chamber before that enormous eye.

The eye opened. Its terrible light fell out upon them. Amos felt the cold heat of it, the scintillating provocative pain of its touch. It felt all around the human parts of him, his pain, his tender memories, his wife's touch, his mother's smile. As the eye witnessed these things, so did he witness them. He wailed as the eye dismissed them and they burned away from him. His skin sizzled, ran and dripped off him.

When he finally stood up before the eye with his children, he did so on new legs. He looked out through the world from new vertical pupils. His forked tongue flicked out and tasted the air of this ancient sanctuary.

Truth had come at last. He understood. His people had once ruled this great planet, they had travelled out among the stars, and eaten of the fruit of conquest. Their enemies had been many, however, and they had tricked them. They poisoned their seers, those who could pilot their living ships across the heavens. They were cast down to cower in the dark earth that was now strange to them, and filled with apes whose very existence was a mockery.

They built a great mind inside the mountain that could care for them, govern them, keep them safe through the long millennia. Calculations had been made, and a new hope was discovered by the mixing of the patterns of reptile and ape. Someday, a new seer would be born, a liberator, who would breed a new era. Their people would once more rise out of their caverns and retake the Earth. They would spread their seed across a thousand galaxies.

That seer had come.

The cavern floor swarmed now with reptilians, eager to see their new queen. Their eyes flitted over the one who once was Amos, and they hissed their congratulations.

Your story will live forever in the annals of our people! A great cacophony arose, and then built to a single note.

The one who had been promised, she who was born Miriam, but would be henceforward named Liberator, rose above them, and they hissed their approval at her ascension.

~END~

The Visitor
By Bruno Lombardi

Absalom Stoltzfus was about two seconds away from having his buggy run over the man on the road when he noticed that he was, in fact, still breathing and *not*, as Absalom initially suspected, a Returned.

That would have been *awkward*, to say the least.

In retrospect, Absalom realised that everything about the man marked him as far away from being a Returned as possible.

His clothes were, of course, a big hint. While obviously those of the (now gone) *Modern* world, they were in remarkably good condition. Certainly cleaner and less ragged than what the Seekers were wearing these days. Perhaps the man had found an undisturbed cache of clothing? But that was rather unlikely, especially after—what?—fifteen, sixteen years now.

The man was also looking much healthier than one would expect for a Seeker or for one of the rumoured so-called Forest Dwellers. In fact, the man looked positively... chubby. His hair was perfectly groomed and, most unusual of all, he was clean-shaven.

He was lying in a circle of burnt and disturbed debris some twenty feet across. Right in the middle of the road.

Most peculiar indeed thought Absalom.

Taking a quick look to make sure there were no Returned nearby, Absalom, with some difficulty, picked up the man and put him in the back of the buggy.

With a shout, Absalom got his horse moving.

35

* * *

It was two hours later when the man woke up, screaming.

Absalom lived alone—his wife and children were long gone, victims of time, disease, Returned, and other dangers—so calming down the man was a difficult task. Eventually, with some perseverance and luck, the man stopped screaming after a half hour...

...And then promptly fell asleep.

Two hours later, the man woke up again, and this time he stayed awake.

"Where am I?" croaked the man, this time rather more coherent than he'd been earlier.

"Holmesville, Ohio," said Absalom, absently scratching his beard. "How did you get here?"

"I was going to ask you that question," replied the man trying—and failing—to raise himself from the bed. "I remember... bright light?"

"I saw no such light," said Absalom. "But then again, you appeared to be lying on the road for quite some time."

The man grunted and tried once more to raise himself off the bed, this time with slightly more success. "Thanks for finding... Wait a minute," said the man, blinking furiously. "I'm in... *Ohio*?"

"Indeed."

"But... I... I was... in Houston..." stammered the man.

That surprised Absalom. In point of fact, Absalom not only found that immensely surprising but quite *impossible*. He remained silent but his face betrayed him.

"What?" said the man, as he struggled to get up off the bed again, failing once more. "What?"

"My dear sir, Houston was destroyed and swallowed by the waters of the sea over ten years ago."

"WHAT?" screamed the man, almost succeeding in getting out of bed this time.

"I speak the truth, sir. Houston no longer exists. In point of fact, many of the cities no longer exist. They were all destroyed in the Event or in the aftermath."

"The… what?"

"The Event," said Absalom, patently. Outwardly he was calm, but inwardly Absalom was beginning to develop concerns. Was this a madman? "It was fifteen years ago? Remember?"

"Remember *what*?" screamed the man, as he managed, with some success, to finally get out of bed and stand up hesitantly. "What is *going* on here? One minute I'm celebrating New Year's Eve, the next I'm here."

"Sir," replied Absalom, choosing his words carefully. "New Year's Eve was almost three months ago."

"What?" said the man, flatly. "You mean it's *already* 2004?"

There was a long pause as the two men stared at one another in silence. And then –

"Sir – it is *2019*. I… I think you best sit down."

* * *

Absalom found it the most confusing hour of his life.

He was, by the end of the hour, completely and utterly convinced that the man was, as his grandfather used to say, 'touched' in the head. By all accounts, the man—George, by name—was quite sincere, albeit seemingly asleep for the last fifteen years. Well, he insisted that he *wasn't* asleep and that he had been, in his words, "screwing around with his new invention," whatever *that* meant. Nevertheless, he seemed to be completely flabbergasted about what had been happening for the last fifteen years.

"I want to make sure I'm understanding you correctly," said George, as he drank his fifth glass of water. "So I'm going to recap. Fifteen years ago, a comet passed by the Earth."

"Yes."

"And it was…?"

"I believe the term used by the authorities was something involving the word 'radiation.'"

"And the comet made…?"

37

Absalom was on thin ground here. He obviously had no truck with twentieth century technology, let alone twenty-first technology. And it *had* been fifteen years.

"Rays shooting out of com-pu-ters turned everyone staring at them into Returned"

"Returned," George repeated, nodding his head. "And these Returned are *quote* dead but not dead *unquote*, correct?"

"Indeed."

George slowly blinked as he poured himself a sixth glass of water.

"Right," he said, eventually, seemingly to himself. "So, to recap, a radioactive comet turned everyone staring at a computer or TV screen into zombies, and the Amish—for obvious reasons—were the only ones unaffected, so they now control the world." He finished his glass of water in one gulp. "And I travelled fifteen years in time, because, sure, why not."

"You're handling this very well."

"I'm going to faint now."

"Try to fall towards the right. The pillows are softer there."

It was an impressive fall, with its impressiveness reduced somewhat by George falling in the wrong direction. In retrospect, Absalom realized that he should have specified *whose* right he was talking about.

* * *

"And how are we this fine morning?" asked Absalom the next day, as he brought in a bowl of soup for George.

"How on earth can you be cheery like this?" yelled George from the bed, his face buried in his hands.

"I will take that as 'not fine' then," replied Absalom, as he placed some bread and a cup of water next to the soup.

"How did this happen to me?" wailed George, as he stared at a wall in shock. "What am I going to do? How am I going to survive?"

"I know not the answer to the first question, George. That's a question to ask the Lord."

"And the other two questions?" asked George, as he swung his legs off to the side of the bed.

A shovel and a pitchfork landed at George's feet.

"I find working on crops and animals and working with manure a most enlightening experience and one conducive with spiritual and intellectual growth."

"You want me to *shovel* shit?"

"That or leave. With apologies, but I am unable to have you stay here for any length of time without you doing something to earn your keep. I am but one man and am unable to work on the farm and feed and shelter you for any significant amount of time without your assistance."

George's response was just a very long silent stare.

"If it's any consolation, the weather should improve in a few weeks. If you really want to travel to Houston—a journey I advise very strongly *against*—then the roads and weather will be almost bearable."

There was another long moment of silence, and then George sighed and stood up.

"You got some boots, buddy?"

* * *

It was, overall, a pleasant month.

George learned far more about the bowel movements of farm animals then he ever cared to know, he lost ten pounds of fat, gained an inch of girth on his biceps, and had a beard almost as impressive as Absalom's when spring finally arrived.

He insisted, nevertheless, on making the journey to Houston.

It was, by Amish standards, rather an emotional goodbye.

With a backpack full of provisions a new pair of boots, a map, and a sturdy coat, George took his leave of Absalom and walked down the ruined highways towards Houston.

* * *

As the crow flies, it was over 1,200 miles from Holmesville to Houston. However, George wasn't a crow, and the roads were in rather sorry condition after a decade and a half of neglect, so it turned out to be a rather longer distance.

George's stint on Absalom's farm had built up some of his muscles but he was still very much aware of how thirty plus years of sedentary life had made him grossly out of shape. Nevertheless, he was fairly confident that he could maintain a good pace of ten to twenty miles a day. Possibly more if he could bum a wagon ride off some of the many communities—of both 'old' Amish and 'new' Amish—along the way.

With a bit of luck, he anticipated that he'd arrive in Houston in about three months or so.

At least that was the plan.

It turned out to be almost a year before he arrived.

* * *

What surprised George the most was—to be blunt—the friendliness. Yes, there was a bit of hesitation and standoff-ness from the first community he met—understandably so, in his opinion—but that quickly evaporated once they didn't see him as a threat. After that, they were more than happy to give him a bit a food or water or supplies. As he was planning to leave, he noticed that they were preparing for an honest-to-God barn raising.

Well thought George *It's not like I'm in a rush. And they did give me some food so I kind of owe them a favour. And it'll be a good experience...*

Forty-eight hours later, George walked away from the community with a few new bruises and callouses but also a few pats on the back and a promise to deliver a letter from one 'Vernon Yoder' to 'Eli Borntreger' situated three or four villages down the road.

Well, he thought, *he was, after all, going in that direction, so why* not *be a mailman?*

* * *

George ran into his first Returned near the ruins of Columbus, Ohio.

It *really* looked like a zombie, albeit a heavily decayed one. Fortunately for George, the Returned's body consisted merely of a head and a torso, with its limbs long since rotted off. To add insult to injury, it was tangled in the roots of a large oak tree, so all it could accomplish

40

was to growl at George.

George poked it with a stick for a few minutes just for shits and giggles, then ran away when it tried to lunge at him.

George stopped antagonizing Returned from then on.

Fortunately, in the two hundred or so miles from Columbus to Louisville, he only ran into three more Returned and gave each of them wide berths.

* * *

George ran into more and more villages and began staying in each village for progressively longer times, helping out with whatever limited skills he had. They were always open and friendly no matter which one village he entered. He ran into a few 'new' Amish, those who'd survived the Event and managed to be taken in by exiting communities or had adopted the Amish ways.

Invariably he got the same variations of the same tale. The escape by pure luck from the cities, the fact that the vast majority of the Returned decayed within a few months, the reluctant acceptance to the new way of life, the new lives made.

But most of all, he got the same, well, *confession*: they liked their new life. Yes, it was hard, but it was… simpler.

By the time he got to Tennessee, he was staying for weeks at a time rather than days.

There is no rush George kept saying to himself. And slowly—ever so slowly—he began to believe it.

He spent the winter in Arkansas, staying with a family and learning, with some surprise, that he had a knack for repairing buggies.

It was February before he made the final leg.

* * *

Absalom was only slightly exaggerating when he had told George that Houston was destroyed.

It was *mostly* destroyed.

Fortunately, the University of Houston—while definitely worse for wear—was still reasonably intact.

41

With more than a little trepidation, George walked straight to one particular building, and one particular room in the basement... his old research lab.

The machine was still there.

George stared at it, a complex constellation of emotions fighting for control within him. Relief was there, knowing that his invention—one that he had devoted his entire adult life in researching—survived all these years.

But there was also anger and annoyance and resentment, at himself and the machine for being responsible for putting him in this predicament. How was he to know that it could bounce him into some sort of parallel timeline or something?

But there was also... confusion?

With a few repairs, taking only weeks or at most months, the machine would be up and running once more. And it would—in theory, at least—take him back "home."

The source of the confusion lay in the fact that, against all expectations, he was left with one definite feeling—he really didn't want to go home.

This is ridiculous! You're a scientist! And yes, there's no guarantees it'll take you back to your specific timeline! But even with a zero point one percent chance of success, you still have to take that chance!

Right?

Right?

For three days and three nights, George stared at the machine.

And then he made his decision.

* * *

It was—as Absalom later noted—precisely two years to the day since he had found George when he looked up from his porch and saw a familiar figure walking down the road.

"Found what you were looking for?" asked Absalom.

"Yup," George answered.

"And?"

"Got some boots, buddy?"

~END~

Erdvolk Invasion
By Jeff Provine

David had just started the morning plowing when the village bell rang frantic. It sounded even over the grunting breaths of his horse.

He leaned back, pulling the reins around his shoulders and tugging on the handles of the plow. "Abatz, abatz thee!"

Horse, John, snorted and stopped drawing. He stood in one place but pawed the dirt of the field with his hooves.

"Easy, there, John," David told his horse. "I know you're as eager as I to finish the day's work, yet we face interruption."

The horse huffed. David ignored him and unhitched himself, straightening his suspenders and unrolling his sleeves. There was sweat under the brow of his wide-brimmed black hat despite the cool hanging in the morning air.

This far from town, the bell sounded like the ringing of a clock. There was no scent of smoke in the air, so it wasn't a fire. Yet bell rang, on and on.

John shuffled one step to the side. David circled around the horse to pat his neck. "Steady, now. There are bigger things to be dealt with than readying for seed, I've been told."

John tossed his head, throwing his mane from one side to the other.

David laughed. "I agree with you, but don't let it get around too much. We have to look out for the community. Harvest will come in its time."

"Daed!" his son's voice cried from across the field.

David turned. Little Samuel was running toward him. His eyes and mouth were wide. His little black boots kicked through the loose dirt as he went. "Daed! What is that?"

"I don't know yet, Samuel. We'll have to hurry into the village to see."

Samuel shook his head and pointed beyond him, into the sky. "Neh, Daed! What is *that*?"

David felt a cold gust tickle his arms and neck. Was this it? The return of Christ, as promised? After the Death of the English ten years ago, he'd been expecting it almost every day. He clasped his hands and raised them up.

Then he realized Samuel was pointing to the west. David let out the breath he'd been holding. Revelation had been quite clear on Christ coming from the east with the dawn. He would've been late anyhow. Dawn was an hour ago.

Samuel was almost beside him now, both hands pointing. "Daed! It's like a strange cloud!"

David turned and pulled his hat back. The sky was bright blue, as it had been most days after the brown haze of the English cleared up. He imagined whatever they'd left burning had finally burned itself out, and with no engines running for so long now, the sky had been bluer than he ever remembered as a child.

Hanging in the blue was an elongated white shape, a stubby sausage if David had to think of something to compare it with. It moved silently, but even from this distance he could make out the little deck with propellers beneath.

"I don't believe that is a cloud, buwe."

Samuel leaned over, curling up his neck as if that would somehow give him a better view. "Then what is it, Daed?"

"It's a floating vessel. The English called them 'blimps.'" David had seen one himself, during his rumspringa in the city, hanging over the stadium where thousands of people jammed themselves to watch a stickball game. He'd taken a long time in his rumspringa, nearly five years, before returning to the quiet of the community. It'd taken even longer to practice his temper.

Samuel was still a way off from his own rumspringa. David doubted he would see any blimps or much of anything that had gone on before the Death. The world was different now, a wilderness instead of the buzzing hive it had been with motorcars and fast food and millions of English. The boys who went off to run around typically banded together to see if they could make it to other villages amid the decaying waste of the dead English world. Rumspringa had become as much a test of survival as it was of the soul.

David tried not to think of that. "You should've seen a picture of one in your books at schul, neh?"

Samuel stood up straight and looked at him. "Neh."

"Well, you're seeing one now." David patted him on the head. "I'll go into the village and hear what the folk say."

"Shall I hitch up the buggy?"

"No, buwe. You stay here and get John out of his harness. Give him some water and feed. We'll get to the plowing as soon as we can."

"But, Daed, I—"

David looked down at his son and cleared his throat.

Samuel's face dropped. "Yes, Daed."

David left the boy to his work and hurried toward the house. Sara was on the porch, churning as she watched the sky. The bell still rang.

"I'm going into the village," David called

Sara nodded. "What do you think it is?"

David just shrugged at her and marched on toward the road. Already he could see people gathering ahead of him in a sea of blue shirts and black hats. English in their haphazard colors mingled in their place at the back.

The village had grown so much. When the Death came for the English, it had taken so many. Survivors appeared at the village like hungry cats for months after. Not all of them accepted the old ways well enough, but what could the community do? Turn them out into the cold?

No, better to let them live as hired-hands in their little neighborhood on land that Old Troyer rented to them.

David joined the crowd, coming shoulder-to-shoulder with Malachi Schrock. The red-bearded man gave a nod. David nodded back.

Malachi then chuckled and pulled his hat back to scratch his high forehead. "This isn't what I was expecting for today. I had planned to sharpen some axes. You?"

David gave him a look from the corner of his eye. Malachi talked so much he might as well have been one of the English murmuring over on the side of the square. But, it helped the time pass. "Getting to the ploughing."

"Think we'll have a good harvest this year?"

"Won't know unless I can get that field ploughed and planted, but I trust der Herr to provide."

Malachi scratched his head again. "I suppose we ought to get in as much as we can. The storehouses from the English are running low."

David grunted. "We can grow what we need. The new orchards will be providing soon."

"Yeah, but I'm going to miss just opening a can."

"That seems to fit your work ethic."

Malachi growled in his throat, which turned to another chuckle. "We earned those cans fair enough. You remember the smell after the Death took the English, wafting in from the city. Smoke, then rot."

"I remember." The smell seemed to fill his nose once again. It made David put a hand to his face. He stopped himself short and stroked his beard. "That was a hard year. We planted then, you could say. Graves for thousands."

Malachi shuffled his boots. "Do you think we should've left them? Minded our own fields instead?"

"Neh," David replied. "The harvest was what we collected from their cupboards. The elders debated it, and it was found fitting. The fields needed a year to be fallow anyway, since the rains were no good. Der Herr provides."

Malachi shuffled again. David was hoping he'd be quiet at last, but he started up again.

"Maybe we should put together more scouting parties, go out and see if we can—"

A blaring horn interrupted him. David clasped his hands. They itched for the grip on the plough.

The white blimp was over them now, growing larger as it descended. Propellers at the back of the small compartment that hung below the enormous balloon groaned with every turn. David could see figures as shadows on the darkened glass. No one in the crowd said anything.

A door opened, and a long rope-ladder fell out to unfurl itself until the last few yards landed against the ground with a thud. Three figures climbed out, clad from head to toe in white.

"Angels?" Malachi asked in a whisper.

David scrunched up his face. "Men. Why would angels need a blimp?"

"I don't know!" Malachi shot back. "And who are you so—"

The men climbed to the ground. They wore white suits, all one piece with hoods over their heads and masks over their faces. The suits were so clean they shined. One of them was carrying a rifle.

Everyone in the crowd leaned over each other to get a better look. David slipped away from Malachi and pushed forward until he had to lift himself up on his toes to peek over Eli Hershberger's hat.

Two of the men pulled down their white masks and rolled back their hoods. One was a white man with yellow hair, grown long and braided into more than two dozen strands. The other was Asian man with darker eyes and darker skin. They spoke to each other in a language that David didn't know. Finally the white man stepped forward and spoke English. "Hello, everyone! How great it is to see you all here!"

David stared at him along with the rest of the Amish crowd. No one said anything more than a mutter.

"My name is Rainbow. I, like you, once lived on the fringe of society. Mine was a forest commune in Oregon. When the EM spike that killed off the modern world ran its course, we thought it was then end of the world. But it wasn't. This is only the beginning!"

"What is he talking about?" Malachi's voice whispered behind him.

David stuck out a hand to shut him up.

"Two years ago, an envoy just like this one arrived from the Pana-Wave Laboratory in Japan. They knew this was going to happen! Their leaders predicted it. Disbelievers called them a cult and wanted them arrested, but the Pana-Wave wisely fled into the hills. They were prepared when the electromagnetic waves that humans had been so careless with turned on them, killing them with the wifi virus."

"Is that how it happened?" Malachi whispered again.

David turned his hand into a fist and waved it at him.

"Now the Pana-Wave is collecting the survivors of the world. They came to me, as we are now coming to you. We will bring together everyone who has survived to build a new world order under our wise leaders' rule!"

The crowd began to grumble. David blinked his eyes until he had to rub them. The lines of light in the darkness behind his eyelids reminded him of the furrows of his field.

One of the elders, Isaiah Yoder, stepped forward. "Thank you, English, for your offer, but we shall not be leaving our homes. You may take those of your kind with you, if they choose to go."

The Asian man beside Rainbow winced.

Rainbow made a dramatic gesture of raising up his arms. "No, no, that won't do at all! We need everybody! That is the will of the leader! It is a new world order. For everybody!"

Isaiah Yoder shook his head, making his long, gray beard wave across his chest. "We only serve the will of the Lord here. We welcome you to a meal with us, since you've traveled all this way, but then it is best you went back to your homes. We'll stay in ours."

Rainbow took a turn shaking his head. "That's not how it works, pops. We're out mapping all the survivors in the world. Soon the transports'll come to collect you. It is the leader's will."

"Neh, English," Yoder replied.

Rainbow looked down on the elder, then out across the crowd, and then to the white-clad people behind him. "You don't have a choice."

"There is always a choice," Yoder told him, "and we've already made ours to follow the Lord's way."

Fire flashed in Rainbow's eyes, and he barked at those behind him. The white-suited man stepped forward with his gun outstretched and then aimed it in Yoder's face.

The crowd broke out in gasps and murmurs. David took a step forward, but Eli Hershberger caught him by the arm. The tall man shook his head.

Yoder didn't move. Rainbow came up beside him, making faces and tossing his head to shuffle the strands in his hair. Still Yoder didn't move.

"Listen, man." Rainbow growled. "The leader isn't as easy going as things were in the Before. He'll use any means necessary to fix this world."

"Perhaps instead of warring to push one man's will, we could work together for the will of Gott."

Rainbow threw himself backward and yelled one word David could at least translate as "shoot." The man with the gun fired, sending a loud boom that shook the crowd. Screams broke out, and several people ran in different directions.

Yoder gave a cry from the ground. He held his head, which spewed red blood over his hand, though it hadn't killed him.

Bile rose up in David's throat. He pushed around Eli Hershberger and stomped toward the men in white. Visions passed before his eyes as he went: the peace of his field when the harvest stood tall, the wide-eyed bodies of the dead English lying where they had fallen beside their computers, Sara and Samuel sitting on the porch in the evening shade.

David dashed the last steps to the man holding the gun. His dark eyes widened behind the plastic. Words came through his white facemask, but David didn't know them.

Just as the man turned the gun at him, David grabbed the barrel and pulled it upward. He wrenched it out of the man's grip before he had time to pull the safety. The man fell back, shouting.

Rainbow raised his fists. "I must warn you: I have trained for over twelve years in the art of Brazilian—"

Before the Englishman could finish his threat, Malachi burst out of the crowd. He tackled Rainbow like a panicked calf, throwing him to the ground and pinning him under all his weight.

Soon others from the village joined the fray, mostly the English newcomers, grabbing the white-suited men and climbing up the ladder into the blimp above. The battle lasted only a few minutes.

"I thought you guys were pacifists!" Rainbow cried, rolling on the ground as if that would loosen the rope that hogtied him. The rope led to the other men, too, jostling them with his every move. One of the Asian men shouted at him.

David looked at the gun in his hands again. With his calloused fingers, he emptied the bullets onto the ground. Their metal casings glimmered in the morning sun.

"You were right," David told him. He pushed down at the hollow feeling growing in his stomach and shook his head. "I've acted in earnest." Then he called to the men, "We should untie them. They aren't animals!"

"I dunno about that," one of the English said in his murky accent. "Comin' here, telling us we're going to get picked up and hauled off."

Others cheered. David shook his head again.

The elders convened in the meetinghouse as soon as Isaiah Yoder's head had been bandaged. The bullet had only grazed him. David didn't know whether the gunman had intended to move the barrel an inch or if it had been God's will, nor did he know how to ask in the man's language.

Discussion lasted only a few minutes among the elders as David held his head in his hands. He was asked to speak once, and he apologized for his brashness.

"But now what do we do with the newcomers?" Eli Hershberger asked.

"Lock them up!" had been what one of the English from the crowd called. They weren't allowed in the meetinghouse now, even though some of their ideas had slipped in.

Elder Yoder waved his hand and long beard that draped from under the red-stained dressings. "No, we don't have jails, nor should we need them. This is our home, not theirs. We must send them back."

"We will have to escort them."

"Who will do it?"

"We could find volunteers among the English, I am certain."

"Can they be trusted to see it out?"

"Then there should be Amisch with them, too."

David sighed. He looked out the meetinghouse window to the edge of the village where his farm stood. Sara and Samuel would be there, waiting on him to come home. Yet he had to ensure that there would always be a home for them.

He raised his hand and said, "I'll lead them. I started the fight in my rashness, and I'll carry it through to make it right. We'll take these English back to their homes and speak with their leader to explain our ways."

"And I'm with you!" Malachi Schrock said.

David smiled at him and nodded. For once, it was good to hear his impulsive words.

The elders murmured and nodded. Then the rest of the men joined in. Soon members called out offers of supplies and taking over his chores while he was gone. David thanked them each, though his heart ached at being without Sara and Samuel for so long.

If he was able to return at all.

~END~

Amish Rule the World

Good Work Well Worth Doing
By Dave D'Alessio

The horrible atomic bomb of Harry Truman, to give him his English name before he was baptized Hariold Wahrmann, taught the world peace was the only possible future for humanity. It was a powerful lesson, we were told, the price of it paid in myriads killed and the cancers that ravaged survivors.

They came to we Amish and asked us the way. We said, "Follow the teachings of Lord Jesus and Jacob Amman: live simply, do unto others as you would have them do unto you, and follow the Ordnung, the rules of your community." We told them the desire to rule others was the way of the English, the people who were not of the Amish; the way of the Amish was to rule no one but one's self.

The people of the world chose to live simply, as Lord Jesus and Jacob Amman taught and as we Amish had since Jacob's time. People became modest, keeping themselves from the sins of vanity, luxury, and sloth; they toiled simply, cared for one another, and turned the other cheek to any who might slight them. They worked six days a week with simple tools that occupied their hands, and rested on the Sabbath.

Cities that once stank of garbage and exhaust were deserted, their skyscrapers torn down for the stone and steel they were made from. Fertile fields sprouted crops of a hundred kinds and those that once stood barren were filled. Eleven billion people worshiped the Lord and lived by His word.

But a relentless mathematics was known to us. The Lord told us to go forth and multiply, and so we had. But there was only so much land on Earth and only so many crops she could provide. It was proven arithmetically, but the proof was not needed; our people might not be interested in equations, but they could see the fields and count the heads and know: starvation was coming, unless more land was found.

I was the youngest son of four and unmarried, which is why each morning I shaved my face clean. My father was still strong and hale; I was not needed on our farm. And when I showed interest in machines and metalwork and the mathematics of mechanics, I received permissions from my father and my bishop and my elder to take the train to a school in upstate New York still keeeping the unspellable English name of Rensselaer. It was there I met Professor Jörg Lowe and my classmate Neil Armenstark and others who looked up at the night sky, and said, "God has made all this. Should we not discover His mysteries in it?"

We explored the ways and means of discovery. Telescopes were encouraged, as the making of mirrors and lenses was a craft requiring much practice and great concentration, good work well worth doing; that done, we charted the heavens for nights on end. We talked of ways to reach the planets, of stairways through the sky and sketched space elevators in the blank pages of notebooks.

"Reach the planets I believe we must," Professor Lowe said. "The Earth's land is increasingly scarce, but the rest of the Solar System is yet empty. If God so wills, we shall make use of it, and for that we must have a rocket."

Robert Goddard's papers were opened to us, and a professor who had known Werner Braun, once known as von Braun, sent transcriptions of his notebooks. From Russia came the journals of Georg Kohler; when he was among the English he was known as Sergei Korolev and had worked on rockets as well. "You may have them with the blessings of the Lord," he wrote inside the cover of the first, and I later learned that Kohler was a fisherman now and no closer to rockets than the cast of a line into a river.

Neil said, "The best place to build a rocket is on the Equator, where the Earth's rotation imparts maximum velocity to a launch," and we agreed. We thought of Ecuador, whose high mountains would be a step closer to the heavens, but great cities like Brazil's Belém and Suriname's Paramaribo were on flight paths there. Mogadishu met many of our needs, but lacked access to raw materials; Christmas Island was the safest location, but far too remote.

Brazil, though, had her mines and her forests. Recife was a large port not far from the Equator; Professor Lowe tapped his pipe on the map and said, "Let us build it there."

*

I was sent ahead, for my speciality was engine design and until we built the site there would be no building of engines. On the sailing ship to Recife I studied Goddard's plans and learned the way of making rope. In the time of the English I might have taken an airplane and arrived in minutes, but I would have learned nothing.

Brazil felt hot and humid. Even with my coat off and wearing my summer straw hat, every night sweat soaked the armpits of my plain white shirt, and I washed it daily lest it become stained. My wool trousers were too heavy, but in Recife a new brother, Oskar Müller, loaned me a pair in plain linen. He was a forester, and we worked together to clear a field for our rocket's launching pad, sweating in the hot sun side-by-side as we hewed trees to the ground and pulled their stumps with a team of horses. It was good work well worth doing.

Müller brought his family, three fine daughters, twin boys still knee-high and his wife, and so it was simple in the early days: Müller and I cleared the land; Frau Müller taught the children; the Müller girls cooked and cleaned and watched the boys, and the youngsters brought water and gathered kindling.

Neil arrived, and with him his wife and two little ones, and four more families. The surveying stopped while we built proper homes, laying them out neatly along a street we named for Goddard. After the street, we built a school, and after the school a store, and after the store we returned to work on our rocket, Neil on the capsule and I on the engines.

In summer Professor Lowe joined us, entering Recife on an elegant clipper with four masts and sails that gleamed white in the sunshine. He brought with him his wife and his mother, and his four sons, and his daughters, six of them grown and looking for husbands. Lowe was our elder now, and we were a complete district as he also brought with him a bishop, a stout man named Tobias Engles.

Engles met me with a stern look. "I know the way builders can be," he said. "They can let their pride lead them into the ways of sin. I will be watching you, Johan Tal, and will ensure that the good Lord above looks upon you favorably."

*

Our community grew as people who felt they could best serve the Lord Jesus working side by side with us came to live there. Smelters of iron and makers of steel arrived, their furnaces heated by tanks of propane from Saudi Arabia and shipped across the ocean in Massachusetts clippers and Korean junks. We built a road to Recife, and wooden tracks for our carts and carriages drawn by horses, and with the horses came farriers to shoe the horses. From deep in the heart of Brazil came people who understood the ways of jungle spiders. They showed us the means of harvesting silk and spinning it into cables two and three times the strength of steel at a quarter the weight, and they brought their spinning wheels as well.

Our district grew and divided, grew and divided. One new district asked Neil to serve them as its elder and he consented, and so he and I no longer sat up at night, singing hymns and sharing a drop of cider. Another, deeper in the forests, begged Müller for his wisdom, and he went to them as well.

We made all of the rocket we could and with the bishop's approval asked for what we could not make to be made for us. The tanks for fuel came from Pittsburgh and Chicago, the delicate instruments, wound with copper wire purer than we could smelt and drawn finer than we could draw it, from Bern. In China and India skilled people wove delicate cables we would need to control our craft in flight, and from Indonesia came cloth proof against vacuum from which we stitched pressure suits. It was not fast, but it was done in the name of the Lord, and it was right, as it was good work well worth doing.

*

Professor Lowe's eldest daughter Mary was a smart girl who grew into a smart woman, interested in calculus and geometry. We spent long days working with pencil and slide rule, solving the equations of Professor Hohmann, who had described orbital mechanics in so much greater detail than Johannes Kepler. When we together reached the bottom of the page and each of us arrived at the same answer, I went to Professor Lowe.

"I ask permission to marry your daughter," I said.

He said, "It is God's will."

We were married, and I allowed my beard to grow, and together we returned to my engines. We experimented with nozzles and nozzle shapes and it proved that making metals able to withstand the great heat was beyond our skill. We turned to graphite and so miners of graphite and machinists to work it joined us. We built them homes, and expanded our streets to include avenues named for Galileo and Oberth and Ptolemy.

Neil continued with the capsule and the control systems it must command; he, too, worked with graphite surfaces strung with spiderweb cable. His task was made harder by the need to make the capsule air-tight, and so he experimented as well: many a cask was submerged in our river and the air pumped from it, the amount of water inside at the end of the test the measure of success. Professor Lowe stooped over detailed drawings of the entire ship, calculating weights down to the ounce in the margins, his handwriting growing shakier as his years bore more heavily and his eyesight failed. Soon his eldest son, Mark, joined him, and from then on the handwriting was firm and clear.

Once we had done what we could, we sat down for Sabbath and feasted on fried chicken and roast pig and sweet corn we had grown flavored with butter we had churned. While the youngsters ran about, kicking a football, we lit our pipes, Neil and Mary and I, and Mark and his father. And Bishop Engles joined us, for he was desirous of our company and we of his advice.

"We have learned all that can be learned," Professor Lowe said. He watched the field in front of him, where Mark's second son made a ball dance on his foot and head before passing it to Neil's eldest. "The time for experimentation is done. The time for construction has come."

Bishop Engles puffed on his pipe. He was more supportive than he had first seemed, but he was rightly insistent that all would be done properly, with the threat of shunning to those who would not. "You will involve the community," he said. "It would be an act of vanity for you to take this on yourselves."

"Of course," Neil said, and I as well. In truth, we had never thought to do otherwise.

Professor Lowe was still watching the children playing, and we wondered if he had dozed off, for he had reached that age. But a stream of smoke escaped his lips. "There is still the matter of a pilot," he said.

I looked at Neil and he at I and we at Mary and she at us. There were only a few candidates, for only those who were young and strong and who had been involved from the beginning would have the knowledge they needed. Each of the other workers only knew what they had done, the foresters and carpenters their wood, the smelters and mechanics their steel, the miners and machinists their graphite, the spider herders and spinners their silk. There were only Neil and I and Mary, we three and no more.

We would not put ourselves forward, for that would be vanity, and that we feared more than failure.

The Bishop knew this, of course. He took three matches from his pocket and snapped one in half, and hid them in his palm. "Draw," he said.

Neil drew and I drew and Mary drew, and we hid the matches in our hands. But I could feel my match, the small splinters at its base where the Bishop had snapped it off, and knew I had drawn the short straw.

*

While Neil and those with him finished the capsule, I and those with me built the engines as Jacob Amman and the Ordnung and Robert Goddard taught us. The plumbers among us managed the fuel tanks and nozzles and combustion chambers, and once they were assembled we framed them in good Brazilian hardwood, covering the sturdy frames with sheets as thin as we could plane them.

On our cobblestoned pad site we built a gantry of the hardest woods we had, and sets of block-and-tackle with a dozen pulleys each so raising an object one foot meant we must draw a rope twenty-four feet, but would lift one twenty-fourth the weight, or so it would seem to us.

And our work was yet not done. We laid out our tables in long rows and dug fire pits and brewed root beer by the tun. And when all was made ready dozens of our friends from nearby districts came to visit, and we stayed up that night while the young ones danced and the rest of us sang and smoked our pipes and talked about the times we had in creating something never before seen on the face of the Earth.

We men woke at the dawn as we always did, and found stacks of pancakes and bowls of oatmeal waiting for us to say grace over. And once we were done with those, we met outside in the shadow of the gantry we built, the tackle and our strong spider-silk rope hanging from it like vines from the jungle trees.

It is said you must build from the ground up and so we pulled one of our engines to the center of our launch pad and stood it there, held upright by many hands, while we made sure with our bubbles that it was perfectly straight.

Around that center engine we placed six more, each lifted by forty hands, hardwood frames of one secured to the next the way we all knew, with glue made from the hooves of our horses that had died, drilling pilot holes with brace and bit, and screwing them together so tightly that even the strongest of us could turn the screw no tighter. And once we had surrounded the first engine with a solid frame, we sang a hymn of praise and lifted it up and out, to be sure the second stage of engines around it would fall away properly when their duty was done.

It was hot, but many hands make the work light, and we stopped only to gulp down glass after glasses of clear water and cool lemonade. The men took off their coats and laid them carefully aside; the women left their aprons on and we teased them for it, but were secretly jealous as they had pockets right in front of them while we had to reach into our trousers.

Around the ring of six engines we built a second ring of twelve, the first stage of our craft, the stage that would push our capsule high into the sky until its tanks ran out of fuel and it fell away into the blue Atlantic. It was the same but more of the same, many hands holding each engine in place. We measured twice each time before we drilled a hole or painted a stripe of glue or turned a single screw, and once we had measured twice Mark Lowe or Neil or myself would measure once more. And again we checked it thoroughly to be sure it would slip away safely from our second stage, and satisfied ourselves it would.

It was growing late and we were growing tired, but we did not stop, for we still had good work to do and there was still sunlight to do it in. The last engine, the nineteenth, was at the center of the capsule Neil had built; it would let me down to the Moon and bring me back once I was there. We attached five pulleys to the capsule and put thirty strong people on each rope, and together we sang and heaved the capsule to the top of the rocket and set it gently in place.

And then, in the sunset, we stood back to look at what we had done in the name of the Lord. The lowest stage was broadly pyramidal, if a six-sided structure could be called pyramidal. Bishop Engles said the lower structures were to remain plain, and so they were simply stained to preserve them against the Brazilian wet, but, Bishop or no, each was painted with a hex sign to ward off evil.

At the top the capsule was white washed with many coats until it reflected the red of the setting sun. The bishop had not wanted it painted either, but Professor Lowe had prevailed on him, explaining it would keep the capsule cool once it was out of the protection of Earth's atmosphere.

Bishop Engels worked with us, and now he prayed with us. "We give thanks to Lord Jesus for giving us good work well worth doing," he prayed, and it was a good prayer.

We would have stood there for hours admiring our work, but that would have been vanity. Professor Lowe's wife, Mary, for whom my brilliant wife was named, called out, "Let us feast!" And we did until the fires burned low and the light was gone and it was time for us to rest.

*

I do not know how many went home that night and went to sleep, but I know I did not, nor my Mary, nor Neil. "May I visit?" he said and held up a lantern, willing to burn his own oil to light our home.

He was my best and oldest friend, and he had known Mary for as many years as I. "You are always welcome at any time," she said.

She laid out bread and apple butter on our kitchen table, and put the pot on for tea, kindling a fire in the stove from the coals she had banked up inside. And as we waited for the pot to boil, Neil said, "You know you will die tomorrow, do you not, Johan?"

"Yes," I said.

There was no hope our rocket would succeed. The idea was sound, the calculations complete, the craftsmanship as perfect as people who had worked with their hands their entire lives could make it.

But there were too many unknowns, too many things we had not prepared for because we had not done this before and did not know what needed preparing for.

Tomorrow our launch would fail. Neil and Mary and Professor Lowe, yes, and even Bishop Engles, they and all the others would find out what went wrong, and correct what needed correcting, and soon another rocket would be ready for whatever lessons Lord Jesus chose to teach us with it. But this launch would fail and there was no hope I would survive. I said, "It is the will of Our Father Who Art in Heaven, and if it his will that I not die, then I shall not."

Neil looked at Mary. She knew all that I did and held his gaze as firmly as her father would have wished. He looked back to me. "You should let me go."

"It was I who drew the short match, Neil." I will not say it was God's will, for that would be a sin. "It was our agreement, and so it shall be done."

The kettle whistled and Mary took it off the stove to put aside to cool. She placed our best teacups in front of us, but instead of tea leaves and hot water, she filled each with the last of our good whiskey. "Join me in saying goodbye to my husband, friend Neil," she said.

"What shall I do without you, Johan?" Neil was perhaps closer to tears than Mary or I, but we were not far from them.

It pained me to know my going would hurt them so. "You will learn, everything you can, and rebuild, and succeed," I said. "You will go to the moon, Neil, and you need not miss me, as my spirit will be there waiting for you."

And as for me, I would learn those things a man was not meant to learn until he died: which way the scales of his life tilted, whether he would join the pure of heart above or those who sinned below, and what was the True Face of God. For Death awaits us all, and then all our questions are answered.

*

I rose with the dawn, as the habits of a lifetime cannot be overcome by a night of drinking. I ate what Mary set before me, good oatmeal with an egg cracked over it to poach on the hot cereal. When I rose she kissed my cheek and gave me a hamper filled with sandwiches, enough to feed me to the moon and back.

I pulled on the pressure suit made from rubberized cloth. It would keep air inside and work under pressure, and that was all I asked of it.

Neil waited outside, and Professor Lowe, and Bishop Engles, and one at a time they took my hand and shook it. Bishop Engles said, "God speed, Johan Tal," and the others much the same.

The day dawned bright and clear and blue, as the red sky the night before had foretold, and the sun shined on the white-washed capsule, reminding me of the snows of upstate New York. The rocket itself was well-made, as was right and proper for the use we intended it for. If the Lord Jesus saw fit the Moon would one day be land, and good farmland at that, and it would take good plows and good spaceships to make that happen.

The people of the surrounding districts were at work already. The launch might be today, but there was still wood to be cut and trimmed, ores to be mined and smelted, spider silk to be reaped and spun, and so the Lord's good work must be done. There were few people at the launch pad and fewer on the way, and so I walked alone, a crash helmet under my arm and Mary's hamper in my hand.

I climbed the ladder up the gantry and lowered myself into the capsule. It was large enough around to cap the tops of the first stage engines, a thick layer of asbestos protecting me from their flames, and so there was plenty of room for me to stow Mary's hamper in the capsule with me.

There was a window in the capsule, a rectangle of mica fitted in the wall next to my head. Neil decided the best way to speak to me was by smoke signal: simple, clear, elegant, unambiguous. Through the window I could see the signal fire burning; the men tending it fed it green wood, turning the smoke thick and black. They wielded a blanket above it, releasing smoke in agreed patterns. Sixty minutes, they said.

There was a cupboard in reach and I opened it. Inside were the two books I would need on my journey, God's own words in the Holy Bible, and The Martyr's Mirror, the story of those who died for the faith. I opened the Bible to the Revelations of Saint John.

Another signal. Thirty minutes. I read on.

Another signal. Five minutes. I put the book into its cupboard, and latched the door closed. To my right was the throttle; whoever made it sanded it smooth and preserved it with varnish. It was good work well worth doing.

Puffs of smoke rose from the pyre. Ten seconds. The closer we launched to the exact time Mary calculated, the less fuel we would need for steering.

Three seconds.

Two.

One.

I pulled the throttle back, and as its lever took up the slack in its spider silk cables the engines of the first stage ignited. The craft began to shake and rattle, a vibration I hoped Neil was noting.

I pulled harder, releasing more fuel and oxidizer into the combustion chambers of the first stage's engines. The shaking increased and my teeth clicked together. I bit my lip to stop them; there was no point in chipping my teeth if a bloody lip would save them.

The ship lifted free of the ground. I could see it through my tiny window, see the gantry falling away as the thrust of our wonderful engines pushed me back into my seat, see Neil waving his hat from the ground. The ship and I, we lifted above the gantry, above the trees, above the hills.

Weight pressed down on me, the weight of another person, two others, three. Behind me the engines roared, and I counted seconds carefully. The first stage engines would fire for twenty-three seconds and then I would release them to fall into the sea.

One engine sputtered, and another. The capsule started to shake as the thrust became unbalanced. I reached for the release lever, my arm now four times heavier than it had been, but a lifetime of physical work made me able to grasp the wooden handle. I pulled it.

The capsule jerked as the first stage slipped off the second, and again as it failed to clear away. I heard the cracking of timbers, smelled smoke. In my hand the tiller jumped free, the cables attached to it snapped. The ship spun sharply, toward the ocean.

I had the feeling of floating free, and wished I had eaten one more of Mary's sandwiches.

The ship threw me against the capsule's beams.

Bright pain exploded.

I looked into the face of Our Lord Jesus Christ and knew all was right with the world. I would wait for Neil at the moon.

~END~

Catherine and the Wild Boar
By Barbara Austin

January 1991

Catherine extinguished the candle and left her cottage.

Outside, the air was thick. Her face felt wet, although the rain had stopped. The puddles filling the ruts in the road were as smooth as polished gems. Shivering, she pulled her cloak tighter. The sagging gray clouds heralded an early nightfall. Usually, she liked the sweet, smoky smell of turf burning in the stoves of the houses she passed, but lately the odor nauseated her.

The ground grew soggier the closer she came to the fen. She heard a violent rustling in the shoulder-high reeds. Her heart raced. Not a wild boar, she prayed.

Cautiously, she parted the reeds and peered into the gloom. A crane stood on its two spindly legs, the tail of a mouse wriggling in its beak. Catherine watched the bulge in the bird's neck slowly descend.

She circled around the crane. The ground was treacherous. She stopped, recalled the stories, the warnings to stay away from the bog.

Twilight faded into night. She inched forward, testing the ground with a foot before putting down her weight. The spot where women disappeared was on the other side of the fen. Only their clothes and their shoes left behind in a heap in the reeds. She couldn't make it that far before darkness swallowed up the landscape. Another day, then. She felt an unexpected lightness of heart. Today would not be the day.

*

The pearly morning light woke Catherine. She rose from her bed and opened the shutters, letting in a rush of freezing air. After pulling on her cloak, she pinned up her hair and covered it with her prayer cap.

The turf fire smoldered in the center of the room. She poured water from a clay pitcher into a pan and set the pan on the fire. When the water boiled, she threw in a handful of dried rosehips to steep. She sat at the table, unwrapped the cloth from her loaf of bread, and tore off a hunk. After saying a silent prayer, she raised her eyes and let her gaze linger for a moment on her father's empty chair.

Someone pounded on the door.

She slid back the bolt.

The man standing on the step was tall with narrow shoulders. He wore a wide-brimmed felt hat over his long, orange hair. His beard was thin. It wasn't unusual to find the preacher on her doorstep with a message from the bishop.

"Good morning, Preacher Wouter. Please come in. Would you like a cup of tea?"

He stripped off his plain wool coat, folded it over the back of her father's chair, and sat down.

"I'm sorry to disturb you at such an early hour."

She nodded and waited for him to state his business. Wouter had opposed her appointment as scribe, the position left vacant upon her father's death. He had taught Catherine everything he knew, starting when she was a child. When she applied for the position, the bishop gave her three tasks to complete: translating a letter from German to English, translating one from French to German, and copying over fifty pages of the New Testament.

She had worked late into the night with the light from a candle, her eyes red and sore, and she finished the tasks in ten days. The bishop approved her appointment. She was the first female scribe in the congregation's history. No one inside the Lowlands came close to matching her skills, but she couldn't afford to be complacent. She practiced writing. She wrote about daily life in the village, about the sorrows and the frolics. It was against the rules to possess manuscripts unrelated to official Church business, so each evening she burned what she had written.

"Does Bishop Cornelius have a task for me?" she asked.

Wouter opened a leather satchel and handed her a letter.

"This arrived late last night. The bishop needs it translated at once."

"Do you mean *now*?"

He paced the small cottage, three steps one way, three steps the other.

"Read it out loud. You can transcribe it later at your leisure."

Trembling with excitement, she heated the blade of a knife in the fire, then slid it under the wax seal. The letter was dated 6 January 1991, a week ago.

She translated aloud:

Dear Cornelius, Bishop of the Rein Order,

I am sending Preacher John of the Southern Congregation of the British Isles to speak to you about an urgent matter on my behalf. An interpreter will accompany him. They will arrive on the Queen Anne and disembark at the port of Utrecht on the 14th of the month, barring unfavorable weather. Please arrange for a trusted servant of the Ministry to welcome them, supply two sound horses, and escort them to your fair village of Amerongen. I wish your congregation allowed telephones so we could communicate more speedily, but I respect your views. Preacher John and the interpreter will practice the old ways for the duration of their visit in the Lowlands.

Sincerely,

Lewis, Bishop of the British Isles.

She laid the letter on the table and raised her eyes.

Wouter pulled on his coat. "I'll go to Cornelius at once. Tomorrow is the 14th. An envoy must leave within the hour to reach Utrecht before nightfall."

After the dikes on the west coast had broken, the sea swallowed a large bite of land, and Utrecht was now a harbor. Only sailing ships and rowboats were allowed entrance. Ships powered by engines were turned away.

"I wish to offer my services to Bishop Cornelius as an interpreter," she said, trying to hide her excitement at the chance to lay eyes on not one, but two outsiders.

Loathing crossed Wouter's sour face, reminding her his son Raymund had competed for the position of scribe and lost.

"An interpreter is accompanying Preacher John. The British might think we don't trust them if we want our own interpreter present, too."

"Officially, I could attend as scribe, to make a record of the meeting."

"I'll pass along your advice to Bishop Cornelius," he said grudgingly.

*

After pottering around the cottage, Catherine pulled a bonnet over her prayer cap, grabbed her shopping basket, and walked to the village in her clogs. Her heart beat at a joyful pace; there was a spring in her step. She hoped Cornelius would take her suggestion to heart. The draw of the forbidden bog weakened.

Her first stop was at the greengrocer's.

He leered at her before filling her basket with the limpest carrot, the most wilted cabbage, and potatoes with bulging sprouts. But he charged her as much as for his finest produce. She swallowed her anger and mumbled a thank you.

She passed the village smithy, the weaver's house, and the apothecary before arriving at the shoemaker's shop. The bell over the door jingled when she stepped inside.

"Good morning, Mr. Graber."

The perpetual frown on his face deepened. "Your boots aren't ready."

She had brought them a week ago for new soles. The job should have taken the shoemaker only a few hours, and she had paid in advance. Her hands trembled with the struggle to practice the values of the congregation: humility, submission, a calm spirit. "When might the boots be ready?"

"I have a backlog."

He was lying. The shelves behind the counter were bare. She turned away to hide the anger flushing her face.

Puddles dotted the dirt street, and mud soon caked her clogs.

Before knocking on the Mullers' door, she glanced around. She didn't want to cause trouble for Petranella. At this hour, her husband Theo would be at work, which meant she could have tea with Petranella without his disapproving glare.

The door opened a crack, and Catherine saw Petranella peer out.

"Did anyone see you?"

"No."

The crack widened and Petranella pulled her inside. The fierce heat from the hearth felt like a blow to Catherine's face.

"Let me take your cloak."

"No, thank you."

"You'll get hot," Petranella said, placing her hands on her wide hips.

"If I do, I'll take it off."

Catherine set her clogs next to the door.

Petranella's house was twice the size of Catherine's cottage. The house had two bedrooms, the small one furnished like a nursery. Theo had carved a crib from a pine he had felled. But Petranella, plump and pink and bursting with health, still wasn't pregnant.

"Tea?"

"Yes, please."

"It does me good to see you," Petranella said. "I was worrying. How long has it been?"

"I was sick."

"I would have brought soup if I'd known."

"I managed. How's Theo?"

"He's a good husband."

"But he forbids you to see me."

"That will change after you take a husband."

"I don't want a husband."

Petranella's hand, warm from holding the cup of hot tea, took Catherine's hand.

"Cat, forget about Simon. He's been gone for five months. Another man can make you happy, give you children."

Catherine winced. "I fear he's dead."

The Ministry had shunned Simon for repeatedly violating the *Ordnung*. He must have died in the forest from exposure or succumbed to a fever. Nothing less explained his long absence.

"More reason for you to marry. What about Hans Schwartz? He has a dairy farm. You would never want for milk or cheese. I've seen the admiring way he looks at you," Petranella said with a mischievous smile.

Hans was kind, both to people and to animals. He kept his barn clean and paid his debts—reason enough to consider him as a husband if circumstances had been different.

"I'm afraid not."

"Oh Cat." Petranella said, her eyes filling with tears. "Don't waste your life mourning a man you can't have."

Catherine pulled away. Petranella disapproved of Simon's rebellious ways, the very aspect of his character that attracted Catherine.

"Thank you for the tea, Petra. I have work to do."

"Do you mean a translation? There's talk that a courier delivered a letter to Bishop Cornelius in the wee hours."

The arrival of a courier in Amerongen always made the populace curious, and gossip traveled fast. Who needed a telephone?

"Preacher Wouter gave me a task. That's all I'm free to tell you.

"Bless you, Cat."

*

It was dusk by the time Catherine finished her chores. She lit a candle and reread Bishop Lewis's letter. Selecting the same shade of blue ink, she formed her letters as her father had taught her, making them both legible and pleasing to the eye. The translation would be filed in the Church's dusty archive, never again to see daylight. But she felt honored to have her manuscript included among those of the scribes who had preceded her going back to the 1700s.

*

The next night, the click-click of horses' hooves woke her. She opened the shutters a crack and peeked out. The shadowy figures of three horsemen rode in single file past the house, picking their way along the dark, muddy ruts. She guessed these were the men traveling from Utrecht.

It was daylight when Wouter rapped at the door. This time he refused her offer of tea.

"The bishop requests your attendance at the meeting with the British."

Catherine suppressed a smile. "What time, sir?"

"One o'clock. Be prompt."

"Of course."

"Beware of the sin of pride," the preacher warned.

She felt her face glow as red as a smoldering brick of turf.

*

The bishop's brown brick house was the biggest in the village. An extension at the back housed Cornelius' library. He had made his fortune by developing a fungus-resistant variety of tobacco. He divided his time between Church business and scholarly study. His book collection was unique in the Lowlands, containing books produced in Germany on printing presses instead of written by hand. He traveled to Germany several times a year to be apprised of developments in the outside world and to meet with foreign petitioners.

Sarah, the bishop's wife, showed Catherine into the living room. Tendrils of white hair framed her kind face, straying from under her prayer cap. The dress she wore was plain but made from the finest wool. Catherine felt boorish in her grimy cloak.

73

Sarah said, "You look more like your mother every time I see you."

"I wish I could remember her."

Sarah squeezed her hands. "I'll tell Cornelius you're here."

A few minutes later, Catherine heard footsteps on the staircase. The bishop was ninety, frail, and almost blind. During his fifty-year tenure, he had approved new inventions for use outside of the Rein Order, while preserving the old ways in the Lowlands. Her appointment was one of the few exceptions. Nights, she lay awake worrying about how her life would change after his death.

Cornelius entered the room, leaning on Sarah's arm. The bishop lowered himself into a chair while his wife arranged pillows behind his back. Smile lines crinkled the skin around his eyes and mouth. But she knew he was a strict disciplinarian. Unrepentant sinners were shunned.

He said, "Take off your cloak, Catherine."

"If you don't mind, I want to keep it on. I'm chilled to the bone."

"I'll lay another brick on the fire," Sarah said.

Catherine sat down and eyed the two empty chairs. She wondered when the outsiders would arrive.

"I miss your father," Cornelius said. "He was my friend and my scribe."

"I miss him, too."

"I'm glad I could help by appointing you scribe."

She nodded. The position was hers while the bishop lived. After his death, she would be dependent on handouts from the congregation. They wouldn't let her starve or want for a roof over her head, but she hated needing charity. Yes, she was guilty of the sin of pride.

Footsteps stomped on the front porch.

An icy wind entered with the men, making Catherine shiver despite her cloak. Preacher John was balding and had a curly, gray beard. He hobbled inside, maybe because of the long journey on horseback. The young interpreter had a mane of chestnut hair. His beard was short, which meant he had married recently.

She gaped. The way he cocked his head. The cowlick just right of center on his forehead. Their eyes met. Simon Bakker! *Her* Simon. But Preacher John introduced him as Steven Smith. He had changed his name, gotten married, grown a beard—all in the space of five months. Cornelius didn't seem to recognize Simon, but he had met him only once before, and his eyesight was poor.

Sarah served coffee with thick cream. Catherine burned her tongue on the first sip, but she scarcely noticed. Her head buzzed. She couldn't think. Simon was alive. He had come back, but not to her. His beard mesmerized her. Blondish red, a lighter color than the chestnut hair on his head.

She had given him English lessons in her little cottage. He was a fast learner. She thought back on the sweet afternoons in bed after the lessons. She recalled her sorrow when Cornelius shunned Simon for punching the shoemaker's son in the nose. And before that, he had beaten Theo with a hammer. Simon had a temper when thwarted. But Cornelius had given him the chance to repent, make amends, and rejoin the congregation. Instead, he fled. He left Catherine. He married someone else.

"Shall we begin the meeting?" Cornelius said in his native German.

Simon took his cue and translated Cornelius' words into English.

Preacher John listened to Simon, then cleared his throat. "Thank you for agreeing to receive us on short notice."

Being fluent in both languages, Catherine scarcely heard Simon's translations, and bent her head over her notes.

"You are most welcome. How can I help?" Cornelius asked.

"I bear news from America. The land is on the brink of civil war," Preacher John said.

"War? How can this be?"

Cornelius' shock was understandable. There hadn't been war since the Church came to power three hundred years ago.

Preacher John took a sip of coffee before replying.

"As you know, trains connect the major cities across America. Most households have electricity and a telephone. Women have been assimilated into the workforce. Computers are increasing productivity. You yourself gave approval for these innovations."

A pained expression crossed Cornelius' face, but he said nothing.

The British preacher continued. "America is divided over a proposed new information system called the World Wide Web. It will enable users to share information across the Internet. Liberals believe the Web should be controlled centrally by the Ministry. Conservatives favor a decentralized approach in which the individual is empowered."

"The Church values conformity above individualism," Cornelius said.

"That is true," Preacher John said. "But the decentralized approach has merits. The free accessibility could stimulate the sense of brotherhood and help prevent future wars. The free flow of ideas and information could lead to innovations that benefit humanity."

"What innovations?" Cornelius asked.

"Finding the cure for diseases, for example."

Catherine didn't understand the nature of the *Web* or the *Internet*. What, for God's sake, was an *information system*? But she was hungry to learn.

After a long silence, Cornelius said, "What kind of violence?"

"Beatings. Riots. Car bombs. The violence is escalating."

Cornelius' face had turned gray. He groaned.

Sarah rushed to his side.

"Please go now," she entreated her guests. "My husband needs to rest."

Cornelius held up his hand. "Wait, Sarah. Our guests have made a long, arduous journey. What do you want from me, Preacher John?"

"We fear the British Isles will suffer a similar fate. Already, the people are divided over the same issues. But if you—the Bishop of the Rein Order—sanction one approach and forbid the other, the congregation will obey and further violence could be averted."

The British preacher spoke in that vein for several minutes.

Cornelius listened to Simon's interpretation. Then another silence fell, broken only by the hiss of the fire.

At last, Cornelius stirred. "I must confer with the Ministry. Come back tomorrow for my decision."

Catherine rose and waited for the two visitors to don their coats and head for the inn where a warm fire and a hot dinner awaited them. She set out for her cottage halfway up the muddy hill. Clogs were practical, but she wished she had on her attractive leather boots. She wished she had looked her prettiest for Simon. The sin of vanity, she chastised herself.

The sky darkened, and the wind drove rain slantwise across the path. Her cottage was dark and stuffy. The smell of the smoldering turf was overpowering, but she didn't dare open the shutters. Boys from the village had thrown rocks and broken the glass. She couldn't afford new panes.

She wanted a hot cup of tea, but the water jug was empty. The well her father had dug wasn't far from the cottage. Still bundled in her wet garments, she picked up the jug and opened the front door. A figure on the doorstep startled her, his fist raised to knock. He wore a long coat and a wide-brimmed hat. His face was in shadows. But she would recognize him anywhere.

"Aren't you going to invite me inside?" he said, as if he had left her only yesterday.

She hesitated, undecided whether to push past him or to slam the door in his face.

He pried her fingers from the handle and carried the jug to the well. She watched from the doorway as he pumped water. She longed to feel his powerful arms around her, but he had a wife overseas. An image of the forbidden bog floated before her eyes, calling to her stronger than ever.

Simon returned and walked past her into the cottage. He discarded his hat, his dripping coat, and his muddy boots. He threw a handful of dried rosehips into the pan and set the pan on the fire. Soon the tea was bubbling. He strained it into two cups and sat at the table. Her longing turned to anger. He knew she was forbidden to drink tea with a shunned member of the congregation.

"I understand," he said. "You can't eat or drink with Simon Bakker. But the Ministry didn't shun Steven Smith."

He was twisting the truth. But a flimsy excuse was all she needed. She sat and drew the cup to her.

He reached out and removed her bonnet. Goosebumps prickled her skin when he removed the prayer cap, uncovering her hair.

"That's better," he said.

"I thought you were dead."

"I'm sorry, Cat. But being shunned made me realize how much I hated living in the Lowlands. I hated the old ways, the hardships disguised as virtues. So I stowed away on a trading vessel bound for the British Isles. I began a new life in London. But settling in America someday is my goal."

He reached for her hand, but she drew back.

"I've missed you," he said.

"You married fast."

"My wife is Preacher John's daughter. When she became pregnant, I had no choice but to marry her. I'll be a father before summer. But it's you I love."

"I would have gone with you," she said, her voice breaking, her heart breaking for the thousandth time.

"The journey is too dangerous for a woman."

She said nothing, not wanting to humiliate herself. Too proud to weep in his presence. He had used her.

"Why did you come back?"

"It might be my last chance to see you."

Her face felt hot. She wanted to believe him. But it was more likely he hoped to advance his prospects with the Ministry.

"What if you're recognized?" she said.

"I don't intend to visit my kin in Leersum, and I'm not worried about Cornelius. He's blind. And Wouter hasn't once looked me in the eye. He thinks an interpreter is beneath his notice."

"I know what you mean," she muttered.

"Enough talk about me," he said. "Is anyone courting you? Does the dairy farmer still have his eye on you?"

"My work for Cornelius is satisfying enough."

Simon rose from his chair and walked around the table. Standing behind her, he placed his hands on her shoulders. She stiffened. He started unpinning her hair. She didn't stop him. Her hair cascaded to her waist.

"No woman in the British Isles has hair this shade of gold. I should know, because my eyes seek such hair in every crowd."

He was a flatterer and a liar, appealing to her vanity, to her pride. He had changed his name, and she knew neither Simon nor Steven. His warm, rough hands slid inside her cloak and glided over her breasts. Her jaw clenched as his hands slid further down her body. Then he recoiled and jerked back. She drew her cloak tight.

After a moment, she twisted round to face him. He took a step backward. She saw the question in his eyes. But, to his credit, he didn't insult her by putting it into words. It didn't surprise her when his expression hardened and he started pulling on his filthy boots.

"I'll send you money when I can," he said, yanking on his coat.

He set his hat on his head and strode out the door.

She stayed seated for a long time, as though weighted down by stones.

*

The next day, Preacher John and Simon were seated when Catherine arrived at Cornelius' house. The bishop's bed had been carried downstairs and placed near the hearth. He was wrapped in blankets, his upper body propped up on pillows. His face was sallow, his eyes cloudy. The room was thick with tension.

Preacher John nodded a greeting to Catherine.

She took off her bonnet, but kept on her cloak.

Sarah said, "Catherine, sit next to Cornelius. He wants you to

79

interpret his decision."

Why not Simon? she wondered.

She drew her chair to the sickbed, conscious of Simon's presence a few feet away. Had he lain in bed last night mulling over her condition— her ruin? Did he have any regrets? The fire seemed to grow hotter. A bead of sweat rolled down her forehead and stung her eye.

Cornelius spoke. She leaned closer to catch his words, listened, took notes, let her face give away nothing. He fell asleep as soon as he finished speaking, a sleep from which he might never awaken. She suspected his time left on earth could be counted in days, if not hours. She allowed herself a quick glance at Simon. His face had turned white because both his hearing and his German were excellent.

She translated:

"The Ministry debated your proposal late into the night, and we reached a decision."

Preacher John leaned forward.

Catherine continued. "The controversy over the approach to the World Wide Web is polarizing the congregation. Blood is being spilled. I, Cornelius, am the keeper of the *Ordnung*. I am the Bishop of the Rein Order. We are a small congregation dedicated to keeping the old ways alive. A horse can cross the Lowlands in three days. We don't need cars or trains or any of the new inventions that have transformed life in America. But I digress."

She consulted her notes.

"Centralization or de-centralization? Under centralization, the Church could use the Web to monitor the brothers and no longer have to rely on spies. It might even be possible to anticipate and intervene before a brother has even committed a sin. Information deemed offensive could be summarily removed from the Web. Centralization leads to greater conformity but also to restrictions on freedom.

"Under de-centralization, each brother has free and equal access to the Web. Everyone has a voice. Creativity would thrive. But uncensored information could lead to the spread of falsehoods, envy, and chaos. In the Ministry's view, neither approach leads to peace and harmony.

"The Ministry's decision is that the inventor of the World Wide Web shall be ordered to destroy the code that created this monster."

Catherine folded her hands in her lap.

She had not translated the last part of the bishop's decision, the part that had made Simon's face turn white. Despite his poor eyesight, Cornelius recognized Simon, whom he deemed to be a deceitful and violent man incapable of repentance. The bishop had permanently excommunicated Simon.

Simon gave her a grateful look for not betraying him to Preacher John, his father-in-law. But in protecting Simon, Catherine had betrayed both Cornelius and her position as scribe.

The British preacher said nothing, though disappointment was etched into his face. Protocol forbade him to protest. The time allotted for argument was past. He rose and nodded at Sarah. "Please thank your husband for his decision and for his hospitality. We will leave tomorrow at first light."

*

The cottage was bone cold. The fire had gone out. She felt movement in her expanding belly. She couldn't keep her pregnancy a secret much longer. Cornelius was her only ally in the Ministry. After his death, she would be shunned, and Preacher Wouter's son Raymund would become scribe.

At midnight, the clouds separated, revealing a full moon. Catherine left the cottage and sloshed down the hill. She trudged through the village, pausing before the Mullers' cottage. She pressed her palm against Petranella's door for several moments, then continued along the street and out of the village. As she approached the fen, she heard the reeds rustling. She listened, but heard nothing else except for her clogs in the muck. The wild boars were probably hunting in the forest. Moonlight guided her along the edge of the fen. Mud soaked her skirt when she reached the bog, a forbidden place haunted by ghosts. The bog looked as black as ink, but thicker, less fluid.

She shivered in the silver glow of the moonlight, standing on the edge of eternal sleep—like Cornelius in his sickbed. Wouter would be one of several preachers nominated to become the new bishop. The lot might not fall on him, but it didn't matter who replaced Cornelius. Her fate in the Rein Order was sealed.

As she faced the bog, her despair turned into a yearning for the welcoming darkness. She shed her clothing and stepped out of her clogs. Then a sudden commotion made her turn. A boar—the size of a large sheep—glared at her from a few yards away. A female, judging by the small tusks. The boar's hackles were raised and her tail was erect. The long rubbery nose quivered. Catherine could discern piglets prowling in the nearby grass.

The mother boar growled, protecting her young.

Catherine forced herself to speak in a soothing tone. "Good evening. I'm not here to harm you."

As proof, she took a step backward into the bog. And another. The boar stood her ground, breathing hard. Snorted. The standoff lasted several minutes. Then her tail lowered. The boar turned around and lumbered into the grass.

The mud held Catherine's feet fast. Her unborn child kicked. An icy shudder went through her, shaking her spine. Ideas exploded inside her head.

She could sell the cottage and use the money for fare to America. The land would return to peace once the code that created the Web was destroyed. Dogs fighting over a bone will cease their snarling when the bone is taken away. She imagined the wonderful things she could do in America. Take a train across the vast continent, turn on an electric light, read any book she wished. She recalled Preacher John's words: women have been assimilated into the workforce. She could earn her bread as a teacher, raise her child, and be dependent on no one except herself.

America beckoned.

If only she could free her feet from the bog.

Amish Rule the World

~END~

Racing To Paradise
By Daniel Glasser

Nat Berger saw the catastrophe coming weeks before it occurred. The energy markets, where he earned his living trading, had been throwing up red flags left and right. He crammed his largest hiking pack with freeze-dried food, emergency supplies, and a bag of gold coins. His custom-built, carbon-fiber racing bike would be useless – it couldn't handle the extra weight – so he mounted heavy-duty tires on his two-year-old touring bicycle. The Porsche, his pride and joy? Forget about it. If things got as bad as he anticipated, there was no way he could keep it fueled.

He wrote letters with instructions and placed them in envelopes emblazoned "OPEN ONLY IN CASE OF EMERGENCY," which he hand-delivered to his few close friends in New York. They assumed he was either contemplating suicide or planning to go on the lam with the profits from some not-exactly-legal financial deals. All he would say is, "Trust me. It's for your own good."

When the shit hit the fan in the Eastern United States, a week before Halloween, it was impossible to determine what had caused what. Had the North Korean hackers waited for the hurricane to attack the power grid, or had the damage from the hurricane and the rising sea levels exposed the vulnerabilities that the hackers could exploit? It scarcely mattered. Within hours of the storm, lower Manhattan was under three feet of water. The cascading failures plunged everything east of the Mississippi River into darkness. The communication networks soon failed; stores shelves were emptied. The few gas stations whose pumps still worked were drained of their fuel by people trying to flee, but nobody knew where to go.

By then, Nat had fled Tribeca on his bike. As he crossed the Delaware River from New Jersey into Pennsylvania, passing through the town of New Hope, he heard explosions, followed by screams. His days as a six-figure earner were behind him. But what lay ahead?

It took him nearly three days to travel the two-hundred-plus miles to his intended destination, taking obscure back roads to avoid the desperate caravans and the thugs preying on them. His ride finished outside of a town named Paradise in Lancaster County, Pennsylvania. He was a few miles from the farm where, thirty years earlier, he had been christened Willard Nathaniel Hershberger.

The fading sun was still visible on the horizon as Nat guided the bike into a dense grove of oak trees and chained it to a thick sapling. He shed his pack and started pulling clothes out. He'd selected his outfit carefully: Scuffed brown leather boots, an old dark green flannel shirt buttoned to the top to cover his tattoos, and a pair of tatty brown overalls he'd found at a thrift store. He crowned himself with his black, wide-brimmed, felt hat, the one article of clothing he had held onto from his childhood as the oldest son of a Pennsylvania Dutch farm family. He still possessed his slender farmer's build, but with his clean-shaven face, straight blonde hair cropped into a low fade, and motley outfit, he knew he wouldn't fool an Amish person or even a mildly perceptive Mennonite. That wasn't the point, though. He needed to pass unobtrusively among the modern folk whom the Amish still referred to as "Englishmen."

Nat had chosen to leave the Amish community when he reached adulthood. He'd been back only once since leaving for college, to attend his grandfather's funeral. Even though he'd spent a month of evenings attempting to reacquaint himself with the area by studying Google Maps, it looked different from the ground. He had the offline maps on his phone and a solar charger, but couldn't risk them using here; instead, he took the pages he'd ripped from a Rand McNally and stuffed them inside the bib of his overalls.

The day's final strands of light were fading into the horizon as he reached the edge of his parents' farm. As he walked towards the dark, wood-framed buildings, his feet sank into the damp soil. Horses brayed softly and the air smelled of manure. His head flooded with memories: The morning dew soaking through his shoes when he helped Father with before-school chores, playing tag with his brother David and sister Rebecca on late summer evenings. Only now he felt like an outsider in a way he never had when he'd walked Manhattan's concrete sidewalks.

Nat heard familiar voices as he approached the door. He knocked twice, then entered.

Father was standing by the wooden table, drying his hands with a towel. His long, curly beard had gone completely gray, and his thin face was more lined, but he was still rail thin and stood ramrod straight. He met Nat's gaze with a stare of his ice-blue eyes, but said nothing.

His sister Rebecca had been just a girl the last time he saw her; now she was twenty-one. She was taller, but her round cheeks were still tinged pink. She wore a white apron over her black dress and her hair up under a white bonnet. She had the same piercing blue eyes as Father, but hers blinked repeatedly, unsure what they were seeing. The stack of brown ceramic plates she was holding dropped to the table with bang, but did not break.

The noise got Mamma's attention. She looked up from the stove and her face lit up. She was an older copy of Rebecca, slightly stooped, with wisps of silver hair poking out of her bonnet. She set down the large spoon she was holding and raced up to Nat, taking his face in her hands.

"Nathaniel, ist es du?" she said, in Pennsylvania German.

"Ja, ich bin es, Mamma." Yes, it's me.

Mamma threw her arms around him. She was warm, and smelled of lanolin and beef stew.

"We've heard of the troubles among the English," she said. "Are you back for good?"

"I don't know, Mamma. I don't know."

His brother David walked in from the outside, face wet. He was six inches shorter than Nat with thick brown hair, a ruddy face, and a protruding belly that made him appear as if he could tip forward at any moment. David wrapped Nat in a bear hug, saying, "Nice outfit, Brother."

They caught up over dinner. Aside from a snide remark about whether Nat still said grace before meals, Father was mostly silent. No change there. Nat learned that David was staying at home because his wife had kicked him out, though Mamma changed the subject when Nat asked why. Rebecca was still unmarried and living at home, unusual for an Amish woman of her age. She claimed that the right man hadn't come along, to which Father groused that her older brothers' behavior had tainted the family reputation. Nat avoided talking in detail about his life in New York City. They'd neither understand nor approve, and what was the point? He wouldn't be going back there.

Mamma grabbed Nat's hand and squeezed it.

"I think this is the Lord's way of placing you back you where belong."

"Maybe so, Mamma. But He could have been far less disruptive. I worry how the Englishmen around us will respond if their modern ways are gone for good."

The five of them returned to eating in silence, until David piped up: "So, Nat, have you heard about Sarah?"

Forks dropped on the table. Mamma and Rebecca glared at David. Father stared straight ahead.

"I assume she's married?" Nat said.

"Yes, to Amos King's son Joseph. They have four boys." David said, adding with a chuckle. "The youngest one's named 'Nathaniel.'" He elbowed Nat.

"The King Family," Nat said flatly. "That's impressive."

Sarah. She and Nat had been betrothed years before, and while their relationship was chaste in the Amish manner, they'd been deeply in love.

When Nat decided to leave for college, he begged Sarah to come with him. She feared her father, the local bishop, would shun her, so she remained behind. They exchanged a few letters during his freshman year, but after he got his first "English" girlfriend, he stopped writing back.

Nat laid low for the next couple of days, helping his family with the end of the harvest. He made no effort to connect with anyone, either in the local Amish community or among his friends back in New York. He figured the electrical grid was still down, though they were too far from town to see any streetlights.

Sunday morning was church time. Mamma lent Nat Father's spare suit. "It used to be yours," she said brightly.

Nat was desperate to avoid attending the service. It had been too long since he'd been to one, he knew his appearance would draw unwanted attention, and Mamma would be introducing him to families with eligible daughters. But Father wouldn't hear of him skipping out on prayer. "As long as you're living under my roof, these are the rules."

Nat held back when they approached the church. "In a minute, Mamma," he said, as she tugged on his arm. He'd go in on his own and sit in the last row.

The wooden A-frame building was tiny on the outside compared to the stone Catholic edifices Nat was used to walking past in New York. But it seemed somehow even smaller once hunched slightly and stepped through the low doorway. Everyone turned to look; Nat saw a mixture of smiles, nods, squints, and frowns. He turned and slid into the nearest pew.

David, who was exchanging heated whispers near the front with a stout, red-faced woman Nat assumed to be his wife, strode over and sat next to Nat, patting him on the knee.

"Did you miss this?" he said.

Nat looked around, taking in the backs of the heads, trying to see who he recognized. In the front row was a young woman fussing over four boys of varying sizes on either side of her. He couldn't see her face, but he knew it was Sarah. This was her father's church.

The service began, but Nat's mind was elsewhere. Thinking back to the times he and Sarah had spent together. Walking in the fields after Sunday services, their hands brushing against each other's, accidentally, but not really. How he'd lie in bed at night and try to imagine what her body looked like under her clothes, even though he'd never seen a naked woman's body before. Not even a picture.

He looked around the church, watching the people holding their prayer books, chanting and singing in response to the preacher's exhortations. They seem happy and content. Why wasn't he? He remembered the first time he'd thought about leaving. He was seven years old, maybe eight, and Father had taken him on a trip into town to trade with the Englishmen. He saw an English boy about his age sitting on a bench, holding a small gray box. The boy's eyes were fixated on the box and both of his thumbs were sliding furiously across it. Nat approached the boy slowly, until he was standing behind him. The front of the box was filled with glittering lights, and on it were printed the words "GAME BOY." He could not take his eyes off the flashing screen. Father had to drag him away by his suspenders.

When Nat went home that night, he prayed to God for one of those GAME BOY boxes. He knew he wasn't allowed to have anything with wires, but this didn't have wires, did it? It must work by some other magic. Finally, he worked up the courage to ask his parents for one. *Don't be ridiculous,* Father responded, *the answer is no.* Nat appealed to his mother. *Please, Mamma, please, I've never wanted anything as bad as I want this.* Father grabbed him by the arm and dragged him to the sink. *Boy, when I say* no, *the answer is no.* Father held Nat's head over the sink and shoveled soapy water into Nat's mouth. *That will teach you to talk back to me.* Nat's eyes stung from the taste and the tears.

Years later, whenever he got soap in his mouth during a shower, whether in his Manhattan apartment, the Equinox Club's locker room, or even at the poshest resorts on St. Barts, he flashed back to that moment and was bombarded anew with feelings of anger and shame.

*

When the service ended, Nat rushed outside and walked around the corner to avoid the exiting crowd. A few childhood friends who had seen him at the service approached. As they were leaving, he felt a sharp poke on his shoulder blade. He turned around and saw Sarah.

"So you weren't planning to come over to say hello?" she said.

Her complexion was clear and milky-white, her smile impossibly wide, her eyes lively. A few strands of honey blonde hair escaped her bonnet. Sarah was nine inches shorter than Nat, and as she craned her slender neck to look up at him, Nat took in the expanse of bare skin around her throat. Right behind her were two little boys – Nat guessed around six and four – in traditional Amish garb, with mops of reddish-brown hair and faces sprinkled with freckles, tugging on her dress at the waist.

"Uh, well, I didn't want to bother you," Nat stammered. "You looked busy with the boys."

Sarah narrowed her eyes.

"Samuel, Jacob, this is Nathaniel Hershberger. He grew up here."

The boys nodded and ducked behind their mother.

"Hey," Nat waved to them, then looked up to see a man striding toward them, a wriggling, screaming toddler in his arms. He walked straight up to Sarah and without a word dumped the toddler on her chest. Sarah caught the boy and forced a smile.

"Nathaniel, this is my husband, Joseph."

Unlike Sarah, Joseph was Nat's height, and met his stare. He had bushy, brown eyebrows and greasy hair parted to the side. His beard was red and close-cropped by Amish standards. Nat stuck out his hand, and Joseph shook it with a firm grip.

"I finally get to meet the famous Nathaniel Hershberger. The prodigal son returns." Joseph smiled, and Nat saw that his teeth were crooked and discolored.

"You're a lucky man, Joseph, to be married to this fine woman. And to have these healthy sons."

"I give praise to the Lord every day. Just like my father taught me."

Joseph's smile faded to a scowl.

"Well—" Sarah cut in, "It's a blessing to have you back, Nathaniel. I hope you'll come visit some time."

Nat nodded to them and stepped away. Sarah had done all right for herself, by Amish standards.

*

Nat's friends from New York started trickling into the area over the next several days. They'd opened the envelopes he'd left them, which contained a map and detailed instructions of what to and what not to bring. They brought harrowing stories from New York: Looting, violence, people drowning in the tunnels of the subway. Emergency troops were being mobilized, but the damage was so vast that it would be years, if ever, before things returned to normal.

Nat's friends weren't the only ones arriving in Lancaster County. Word had gotten around that the Amish knew how to function without electricity and were non-violent, so ragtag bands of people arrived from the cities — Allentown, Philadelphia, even Washington — asking for food and places to sleep. The autumn chill was arriving, but the Amish allowed the Englishmen to pitch tents on their land.

"I can't believe you're really Amish," Nat's friend Alistair said to him. Alistair lived in Brooklyn and had worked with Nat on the trading desk; his wife Jessica was seven months pregnant with their first child. Their families lived in California and they had no way to get in touch. "You know, when I first met you, and you told me your name was Nat Berger, I thought, 'He must be adopted, because he doesn't look the least bit Jewish.' Now it all makes sense."

The harvest was nearly over, so Nat helped till the land for winter, and served as an intermediary between the urban refugees and the nearby Amish families. They worked out a set of ground rules: Where to set campfires, when to use the well, how to behave on the Sabbath.

One Thursday afternoon Nat walked over to the King Farm to visit Sarah. It was about seven miles away. He jogged there, in his boots; by the time he arrived his feet were red and hot, and his heels covered in blisters. Sarah's three older boys were playing outside the house. He heard the wails of a toddler coming from inside.

Nat climbed onto the porch and looked inside. Sarah was sitting in a chair, her back to the door; her body was rocking. Two little feet were resting in the crook of her arm. The high-pitched screams paused only long enough for the young child to catch his breath and start anew. Nat stepped inside.

"Sarah, is everything OK?" he asked. She turned to face him. Tears were drying on her cheeks.

"Yes, yes. I'm just trying to calm Nathaniel."

"Is he sick?"

"No. It's just Joseph… He has a bit of a temper."

Nat felt heat rising in his face and his fists clenching.

"Did he hit the boy? Did he hit you?"

"No! Of course not. Joseph is a good provider and a good father. He just needs to yell sometimes. To let off steam."

"That's not OK. You deserve to be treated better."

Sarah shifted her chair so that her body was sideways to Nat. The boy had quieted down and was sucking his thumb.

"That's so sweet. But I'm fine." She sniffled, then smiled. "Never better, in fact. Now, why are you here?"

Nat bit down on his lip before speaking.

"I was passing by, so I thought I'd stop in to say hello. Maybe catch up."

"Now's not a good time," she said, nodding at the boy in her arms. "What about Saturday afternoon? I can meet you by the old mill, near my parents' house. It'll be like old times."

She smiled again, more broadly than before. Nat studied Sarah. He wasn't thinking about what her body looked like under her clothes. He was wondering what she'd look like with makeup on her face, and her hair down, out of its bonnet.

*

Nat couldn't get Sarah off his mind for the next two days. He wanted to know everything about her life and tell her everything about his. Was she truly satisfied? Safe? Did she ever think about him? Did she regret she hadn't left with him years before?

Nat had been waiting by the mill for nearly an hour when Sarah arrived. They sat down next to each other on the log bench where they used to meet as teenagers.

"I don't have much time. Joseph doesn't know I'm here," she said.

Nat desperately wanted to take Sarah's hands in his, as he had once or twice in fits of boldness when they were young. He knew that now this would be too forward. He crammed his hands under his thighs to fight temptation.

They talked for half an hour, but for Nat the time flew by like seconds. Sarah talked about being swallowed up in the large, prominent King clan. How she rarely spent time with her sisters. How much she regretted not having a daughter, but that she was done having children.

"Joseph—and I've never told this to anyone—always, *always* has stinky breath. You can practically smell him coming across the fields," laughing as she confessed. "Not like you. You always smelled good."

"Stop. Just stop," Nat replied. *Tell me more,* he thought.

Nat told her about his life in New York: The money, the parties, the fast bicycles and faster cars. He talked quickly, his stories punctuated only by her gasps, or responses of "Oh, dear!" and "Oh, my!" He told her that the greatest thrill of his life was driving 300 kilometers per hour on the German autobahn. "That's more than three miles a minute!" he exclaimed, before realizing that someone who had never ridden in a motor vehicle would have no concept of how fast that was.

Was he happy there? Who knew? He'd been too busy, too focused on collecting possessions and promotions to contemplate that. But it was moot now. That life was gone. Probably for good.

"And you never got married? Started a family?" Sarah asked.

"I never met the right person," Nat said, "Not in New York, anyway."

Sarah blushed.

"You're not lonely?" she said.

"No! I don't know. I mean, maybe, but so what?" he said. "It's not you can't be lonely when you're married. Right?"

"Nathaniel, I need to go."

"When can I see you again?"

"I don't know." She reached up and brushed his cheek with the back of her hand. "But it was a joy to catch up. I've missed you."

It wasn't much, but it was all Nat needed to hear.

*

Once, when Nat was sixteen, he had headed into town alone on Father's buggy to purchase some supplies. Outside the dry goods store, two English boys were working on their souped-up cars. At the time he knew nothing about cars, but was drawn to the one that was bright yellow. Timidly, he approached the boys and started asking them questions. Before he realized it, they had offered him a ride. He knew he wasn't supposed to accept, but what harm could it do? They took him to a deserted road and hammered the gas. The power of the acceleration was unlike anything he'd ever felt; the closest he'd come was jumping off a cliff twenty feet into a swimming hole. He gushed with excitement. Then the English boy who was driving shifted the car into park and turned to Nat: "OK, Dutch Boy. It's your turn."

As thrilling as it had been to ride at high speeds, it was nothing compared to piloting the metal beast. Nat had never directly felt the presence of Jesus in his midst, but he imagined that this was what it would feel like. When he tried to explain it to Sarah later that day, she shook her head sadly.

"Nat, are you forgetting the Second Commandment? 'Thou shall bring no false idols before me.'"

"Sarah, you have to try it. It will change your life."

"You are succumbing to the temptations of the English ways. Heed the words of Jesus: 'If you continue in my word, you are truly my disciples. Then you will know the truth, and the truth will set you free.'"

"Speed," Nat replied, "Will set me free."

*

It took only a few weeks before the refugees began to wear out their welcome on the Amish lands. The refugees quickly tired of their privation and the constraints their Amish hosts placed upon them. The Amish resented the lack of respect that their English guests showed for their way of life. They feared for the safety of their families and fretted that their stockpiles of supplies would not be enough to last through the coming winter.

The Amish elders talked of calling the local English police to assist them. They might be outsiders, too, but they were a known quantity and had always respected the Amish people's right to live as they pleased.

Nat was caught in the middle, trying to maintain the fragile peace. Meanwhile, he pined for Sarah, plotting for ways that they could be together. Could he convince her to divorce her husband and marry him? If he decided to leave again, could he persuade her to come with him?

He finally hit his breaking point one morning, listening to his friends from New York griping about their situation. *Why did you get us into this mess?* Would they have been happier back in Brooklyn, hiding from looters and avoiding the raw sewage in the streets? He rushed over to Sarah's, his head throbbing in pain, his feet even worse. Why hadn't he thought to bring a stash of Advil and Xanax?

He tried to imagine what he could say to her, but the words weren't coming. Maybe he could serve up a romantic movie line? It would sound corny if you'd heard it before, but it would be new to her.

Nat found Sarah walking back from the water pump, lugging a bucket of water. He caught up to her and grabbed the bucket's handle as he matched her stride.

"Sarah, I need to talk to you," Nat said, in what was almost a growl. "Now."

"You shouldn't be here, Nat," Sarah said, as she kept walking, "People are starting to talk." She craned her neck to make sure nobody was within earshot.

"Listen to me," he said, "I don't think it's going to be safe around here for much longer. If I leave, will you come with me? I can give you a new life. A better life. I promise."

She looked at him, mouth agape.

"What are you saying? What about my family? My boys?"

"We can send for them later, once we've settled somewhere else."

"You can't be serious."

"Look, I know I'm asking a lot. And I'm not sorry that I chose the English life. But now I realize that leaving you behind was the biggest mistake I ever made."

Sarah said nothing. What else could he say to convince her? That famous line from *Casablanca*? He stopped walking and inhaled deeply, then announced:

"If I leave here now and you're not with me, you'll regret it. Maybe not today, maybe not tomorrow, but soon, and for the rest of your life."

Nat felt a hand come down hard on his shoulder and spin him around. He was face-to-face with Joseph.

"What are you doing here?" Joseph said to Nat, then turned to Sarah and, pointing at the house, barked, "Woman, go inside."

Nat stood there. His pulse throbbed in his ears.

Joseph continued: "My father tells me I'm not very good at turning the other cheek. Maybe he's right. But you need to stay off my land and stay away from my wife."

Nat nodded, and trudged away without saying a word. He knew he'd overplayed his hand.

*

It didn't take long for Nat's dire prediction to come true. That evening, a group of young refugee men polished off a case of whiskey that they'd "liberated" from the basement of a bar in Lancaster. Their talk turned to their lack of female companionship, and they decided to seek some out by walking amongst the Amish homes, sing-shouting, "Virgins! Bring out your virgins!" Nat managed to get some of the other refugees to corral the gang and herd them back to the camp at the edge of the Amish property, but the damage was done. Some Amish men came to the camp and told the refugees that they were no longer welcome; they needed to vacate immediately. The refugees refused: They had nowhere to go, and besides, who was going to make them? The Amish, who preached and practiced non-violence, and refused to serve in the military? The sheriff's deputies, who were fully occupied with the emergency response to the power outage and with keeping the peace in the larger towns?

The next morning the Amish elders called an emergency meeting of their community's leaders. Several hundred attended, including Father, representing thousands of Amish who lived in the area. Nat was turned away at the door.

"You're not one of us, Nathaniel," one of the elders told him. "You're an Englishman now."

The meeting lasted three hours. When it broke up, Nat watched the crowds disperse, but nobody would tell him what was decided. Then he spotted Joseph King at the side of the building, grinning and sucking absentmindedly on a long piece of straw. Nat raced up to him.

"Joseph, can you tell me what happened?"

Joseph smiled broadly. Nat winced.

"Wouldn't you like to know?"

"Of course I would."

"Well, I'm afraid I can't tell you." Joseph looked down and spit on Nat's boot.

Nat grabbed Joseph by the lapels and slammed him against the wall. He placed a hand over Joseph's throat and squeezed hard. Joseph, unable to breathe, lifted his hands towards Nat's face, but they fluttered in mid-air.

"Goddamn you, Joseph! Tell me. Now!"

After a few seconds, Joseph dropped his arms. Nat released his grip and took a step back. Joseph collapsed on the ground and coughed furiously.

"You really are an Englishman, *Nathaniel*," Joseph said once he had caught his breath, drawing out the name. "Using violence to get what you want."

"I'm sorry," Nat said. He was panting as well.

"I'll tell you what you want to know, Nathaniel. But you must promise not to divulge this to anyone else. On your honor."

"Yes, yes," Nat said, impatiently, "I give you my solemn word that I'll tell no one."

"I'm sure you will." Joseph smiled before continuing. "It seems that desperate times call for drastic measures, and at least for now, we Amish folk are going to stop turning the other cheek. To fight fire with fire, literally."

The plan, Joseph explained, was to do a controlled burn of the fields where the refugees were camping. This was not common practice, but it was done occasionally after harvest season to speed replenishing the nutrients in the land. Plus, it would scare some sense into the refugees, and more importantly, make the land they were camping on uninhabitable.

"You're lying!" Nat exclaimed.

"If you don't believe me, see for yourself. In the patch of trees near your family's well is hidden a red canister containing the fuel the Englishmen use to run their tractors. Why else would that be on Amish land?"

Nat scoffed as he left Joseph behind. The Amish were frightened and desperate, but they were also experienced and wise, and knew that there was no such thing as a controlled burn of that size. They'd be putting hundreds, possibly thousands, of people at risk. People with nowhere else to go. Women and children. The refugees were a load of trouble, and yes, they needed to move on, but not like this.

But when Nat got back to the Hershberger farm, he found the gas can that Joseph had described. And as soon as he unscrewed its cap, he discovered that Joseph's tip was right.

Nat had promised Joseph that he'd keep the information to himself, and he knew how seriously Amish men took their vows. *A man was only as good as his word,* Father frequently told him. But the Joseph Kings of the world were not the ones to be leading the Amish through an uncertain future. And Nat would never forgive himself if people were harmed and he'd done nothing to stop it. He'd find a way to warn them without breaking his vow.

Nat hurried over to the pasture where the refugees were staying and gathered them together.

"I can't give you details, but you need to tell everyone to pack up and go. You're no longer safe here."

"Hell, no!" one of them responded. "This is nothing but a wily Amish trick to get us to abandon our camp without a fight. We know you're on their side, Berger, or whatever your real name is."

The crowd murmured in agreement.

"Trust me, this is not a trick," Nat said. "If you don't leave, you'll be putting your lives, and your families' lives, in danger."

Somebody cocked a rifle.

"Thank you for your concern, but I think we'll take our chances against these Amish boys."

Nat panicked. Screw the vow.

"Your weapons," he said, "They won't help you against a fire."

"Who said anything about a fire?" a familiar voice called from a distance behind him.

It was Joseph, followed by Amos King and Father, and a group of other elders.

"Didn't I tell you?" Joseph said to the Amish men, "Nathaniel Hershberger is not a man of his word."

"I'm sorry," Nat said, turning to the elders, "I couldn't let you put these people's lives at risk, with that crazy, massive controlled-burn plan. It's literally playing with fire!"

There were murmurs from the crowd of refugees.

Amos King spoke over the crowd: "I can assure you, good English people, that there is no plan to set fires, and there never was. You have been misled by a troubled man, a notorious spinner of lies."

In the distance was a rumbling sound, gradually getting closer.

"Now see, Nathaniel," Joseph sneered, "This has been what you might call a test of honor. And guess what? You failed."

"What about the gas can?"

"One of the Englishmen placed it there. But it was a convenient means of demonstrating your lack of probity."

Nat looked toward the rumbling. A convoy of military trucks approached slowly.

"We asked the county sheriff to call the National Guard," Joseph said, "They'll be relocating these folks to a location that's better suited to their needs. You're free to go with them, but I'm not sure how welcome you'll feel."

Amos King looked at Father. Father nodded at him. Amos stepped forward and faced Nat directly.

"Willard Nathaniel Hershberger, for the offense of breaking your vow to your fellow man, and in so doing recklessly endangering the safety of others, you are hereby permanently shunned from the Amish community. From this day forward, no member of our community may associate with you."

Nat looked over to Father. Father's ice-blue eyes stared back to him, but his expression was stoic, and he said nothing.

"So this is the thanks I get for trying to keep the peace," Nat shouted, sweeping his arm across the crowd of refugees and elders. "Well, fuck you all!"

Nat stormed off.

"That's right, Wil-Lard, run away," Joseph called after him, "It's the one thing you're good at."

After a quarter mile, Nat's feet were too sore to continue. He stopped and removed his boots, and soldiered on barefoot, in a combination of jogging, running, and limping. It took him an hour to reach Sarah's, and he was gasping for breath when he arrived. She was outside, pulling clothes off a clothesline.

"I tried to warn them… your husband… tricked me…" he tried to speak, panting heavily after every few words.

"What are you saying?" Sarah asked, "I don't understand. And where are your shoes?"

Nat finally caught his breath. He drank in Sarah's face. She was effortlessly beautiful. How could he have let her go?

"It's a long story, but I've been shunned," he said. "I'm leaving now. Come with me."

"Shunned?!" Sarah responded. "What did you do?"

"It was Joseph. He set me up. I was just trying to help people. Come with me. Please. I love you. I always have. And I know you love me too. I can feel it."

Nat tried to take Sarah's hands in hers, but she pulled away. Then she straightened up.

"Don't tell me how I feel, Nat. I'm married now. My family is here, and this is where I belong. I know my life's not full of fancy things, but it's a decent, honorable life."

Nat couldn't believe his ears. He was desperate to think of something, anything, to say to salvage the situation.

"How about this? Elizabeth, your sister. She's marriageable. I'll marry her, and then we can be close, even if we can't be together."

"You'd do that for me? You think that's what I want?"

"Sure. I'd do anything for you."

"Or maybe that was your plan all along? Using me to get to my sister, since I'm not young and pretty enough for you after all your fancy English girlfriends. You need one of those Amish virgins your friends were yelling about last night."

Nat fell to his knees.

"That's not true. It's not true at all." He was practically whimpering. "What about us?"

Sarah took a deep breath before responding.

"Nat, this isn't about us. It never has been. It's about you. It's always been about you. *This* is a good life. *I* would have made you a good wife. But it was never enough for you. You've been running for most of your life. Running from your problems. Running from your soul."

She shook her head slowly before continuing.

"You can't stay here. You need to leave before Joseph gets back."

Nat sobbed: "But—"

"Nathaniel, you've been shunned. I can't see you anymore. Ever. Please, for everyone's sake, just go!"

Sarah turned away from him and walked into the house. Nat stared at the door for a moment, then buried his face in his hands.

*

As Nat trudged away, he thought of the fable of the dog and its reflection. A dog with a bone in its mouth is walking along a riverbank. The dog peers into the water and greedily mistakes its reflection for another dog with a tastier morsel. Reaching for the "other" dog's bone, he drops his own into the water and is left with nothing. Nat had forsaken the Amish life for the English life, and then, in his attempt to have the best of both, had lost everything.

It was nearly dusk when Nat made it back to the grove of oak trees, dragging his pack behind him. His bicycle was still there, undisturbed, its tires flat. He filled the tires and changed into his cycling kit. He stuffed his farm clothing into his pack. Except for the black felt hat, which he left lying on the ground as he rode off, alone, to an uncertain destination.

~END~

Harvest
By Shawn Cook

The fog that shrouded the lush green countryside was as absolute as the blank canvas of creation. Rolling fields were little more than vague outlines, the arching limbs of the surrounding forest became jagged lines of frozen lighting. Figures moved in the white, ghosts working their eternal chores.

Occasionally, bird calls and the snorting of plow horses echoed. The distant purr of rubber wheels and humming engines arose in an anachronistic fashion; reminders of a world that never stopped moving forward. The village was one of the smaller Amish communities in the area, established when the state was young.

The farmhouse was large, modest, and sturdy. A single story structure that had withstood years of frigid winter cold and the oppressive midwest summer heat. It had lost not one shingle during the previous springs twister that roared past and devastated the nearest community, Jacksonville, a few scant miles down the road. In the rear, where the large well kept garden lay, Jacob Yoder pushed the tines of the pitchfork deep into the earth and leaned against the handle. Levering back and forth, he worked the potatoes up and out of the rich dirt. The gasp that escaped through his clenched teeth was a sudden and unexpected sound.

Kneeling, he ran his fingers among the tubers and fought the wave of fear that began to creep across his soul.

"...and yet, even more." he murmured in the strengthening light of day. He moved down the row and started again. Tines stabbed, plunged and pulled. More still. Tears rolled down his cheeks, yet he couldn't feel anything but the worn wood of the handle. Onward he continued, and each cluster he unearthed was the same. Sweat matted his hair beneath his wide brimmed hat and his calloused hands ached. The black suspenders chafed his shoulders as he dug.

"How many, Lord?" he repeated.

Just then, a soft hand touched his shoulder with a butterfly grace. "Jacob?" came the voice of his wife, Mary.

He could hear the fear in her voice. He had hoped she wouldn't see...

Jacob turned and gazed upon the woman that had always kept his heart in one piece. She'd been a gift from God, his Mary, and he needed her lighthouse presence more than ever right then.

She gestured behind him at the upturned masses. "Oh, Jacob," she said, "how many, do you think?"

He looked at the piles of rotten and blacked shapes. Shapes that were supposed to be a hearty harvest of potatoes, enough to stockpile. Enough to share with kin and neighbor and still have enough to sell to the English along the road into Hobb's Mill. Instead, each pull had exhumed grinning, blackened and rotted skulls. The largest no larger than his clenched fist, they crowded together and stared into nothing. A slight breeze licked the sweat from his shivering skin.

"All of them, Mary," his voice rasped. "Every man, woman, and child on Earth."

*

Jacob was unsure when Mary had slid his Grandfather's old rocking chair from the house and onto the back porch. He was also at a loss as to when she had maneuvered his numb body to sit and placed a cold cup of water into his hand. He didn't believe he'd lost consciousness; his clothes were no more stained than usual after a morning in the garden, but the last few minutes were nothing more than hazy nothingness to him. He pulled deeply from the cup and silently gazed across the piles of skulls in his garden. Through the open window he could hear Mary fluttering about the kitchen making preparations for what was to come. It would be a long, long day ahead of them and the house would soon have company.

Oh, Jacob, he thought to himself. *Oh, Jacob...this is bad.*

*

Ansom Eader was the first to show, his scraping footfalls announcing him seconds before he peered around the corner of the house. Jacob had almost laughed at the round and red face that stared at him with large owlish eyes. The man's shirt was streaked with sweat, dirt and...blood? Jacob rose as concern for his neighbor flooded his muscles.

"Ans?" he said. "Are you alright?"

The older man brushed aside Jacob's concern with a wave. "Fine, Jacob. I'm fine." He gestured to the drying blood across his chest absently. "It's not mine."

Ansom sat heavily upon the porch and took in the sight of the morbid treasures that littered the garden row. "*Ah*. I see," he said. "Well, now."

Long minutes passed before Ansom spoke again. "That, my friend, is frightening."

"Aye." Jacob grunted. He motioned towards Ansom's shirt. "The blood..."

The question hung in the air. "Well," Ansom replied. "Let's just say that I've given up milk for a while." He swallowed audibly. "Perhaps for good."

"Another piece of the tapestry, then." Jacob said. "Mary is preparing food if you are hungry."

Ansom seemed to pale, as if the thought of food were repulsive. "I'm good, Jacob. I say thanks to you and Mary, but I'm... ah. I'm not hungry."

"Nor I." Jacob replied. "What say we wait here for the rest to arrive? I appreciate the wind on my face right now and have no desire to go inside."

Ansom said nothing, only nodded. The wait was much shorter than they had expected.

The four arrived in various states of shock and disarray. The first to arrive, a beardless young man, named Nathan Uhls, was near catatonic and covered in blood. Only with the help of Thomas Lapp had the youth, no more than nineteen years old and newly baptized, made his path to Jacob's door. Nathan stood trembling and silent, his bright blue eyes rolling wildly. Jacob looked to Thomas questioningly.

"He'll be fine," the old man said. "Once he eats some of Mary's wonderful cooking, he'll be right as the spring."

"And you, Thomas?" Ansom asked. "How fares thy spirit?"

Thomas' eye slid away from the men and gazed towards nothing. "We'll speak in the barn. Until then, I shall see to Nathan."

*

The barn was as expansive as it was tall and pleasantly cool. The heat of the day had yet to raise the interior temperature to an uncomfortable stuffiness. The men sat in silence upon hay bales pulled into a circle. The shakes had finally left Nathan's limbs and the boy seemed to have finally gained some color back into his sallow cheeks. To his left, Thomas sipped from a cup of strong coffee and stared at the ground. Jacob's eyes took every man in, mentally inspecting each and gauging their state of mind.

Nathan was, of course, in the worst shape. Mary had cleaned the blood from his face and hands the best she could. His curly hair was as clean as she could get it only using a bucket of cold water. Nathan's clothes, however, hung like a butcher's smock. Paul Hostetler sat, distracted but little worse for wear, next to the normally jovial Cal Bucher. Bucher's face carried the ghost of a smile, but his eyes were far away.

"Well," Jacob began slowly. "You've all seen my harvest."

"What does it mean?" Nathan spoke for the first time since his arrival.

Jacob pursed his lips. "It means that whatever is coming, it will be absolute. Every living person under God's gaze will die."

"How…? Are you sure?" Nathan asked.

"I remember being a child when Jacob's father foresaw the coming of the Second World War. It was barely a quarter of the yield we've seen today." Ansom replied.

"And I can feel it. Deep into the marrow of my very bones." Jacob said. He looked to Ansom, who sighed and stroked his long beard.

"There was blood coming from the udders of my cow. Thick, dark as ink and reeking of corruption." Ansom paused. "I hadn't noticed until the smell hit me, I'd been thinking of the winter stock and was far away in mind. The smell made me gag and I'd pulled the bucket clear. A bucket full of... horror. I had turned away, sure to be sick, when the cow made a pained sound. I watched as the udder had began to swell and she gave a horrible moan just before it split."

Ansom stopped then, shaking his head at the memory.

Cal grunted and shifted upon the bale. "My rooster killed every hen and chick in the coop," he said. "I was preparing to gather eggs and spread feed when I noticed the silence. It was so still, like an empty church and I had thought that a fox had gotten inside." He took a deep breath. "The rooster was standing there, stock still and staring towards the door. Blood dripped from its beak and coated its comb and feathers. It cocked its head, gave a weak croak, and died."

"I've nothing of that nature." Paul said. "But the water in my well has turned black and smells of sulfur."

Nathan shuddered. His mouth worked like a landed fish. When the words came, they came in a husky rasp. "My horses." he started. "As I was leading the stallion out of the barn, he pulled away from me and kicked down the door to each stall. I tried to calm him, but he wasn't letting me close. The mares and foals approached him, lowered their heads and waited. He went to each in turn, reared up and struck with his hooves, splitting their skulls one by one. In complete silence. Not one horse made a sound. The stallion snorted at me, I thought he was going to charge, but instead he turned. He ran headlong into the far wall and broke his neck."

Thomas removed his hat from his head and slowly rotated the brim in his hands. "I awoke this morning to find a fox sitting at the foot of my bed."

Nathan glanced towards Jacob and opened his mouth to speak, only to close it again when Jacob gave him a curt shake of the head.

"She was beautiful." Thomas continued after a moment. "The red of her fur was as deep as the sunset in summer, the white was pure snow. Her eyes though, were the color of Rebecca's when she was young. Bright green and clear as glass."

He sat silently for a while, the men around him not speaking. Jacob had known Rebecca well, they all had. Before the fever took her a dozen summers ago, she had been a midwife to the village and perhaps one of the smartest people Jacob had ever known. Thomas had been adrift for months after Rebecca had passed and had only seemed to be his old self for the last couple of years.

Thomas cleared his throat. "I didn't move. I was afraid I'd scare her away, but I should have known better. Rebecca had never held fear in her life. She dipped her head, opened her mouth and dropped something onto the quilt." From a pocket he pulled a bright glass marble and held it to the light. It was the blue of a Robin egg with light traces of brown and green swirled through and around. "And then, she was gone."

Jacob could hear the break in the old man's voice, that rasp of emotion that lay dormant but never extinct. Thomas sat still, squeezing the marble in one aged hand and closed his eyes. He breathed deeply once, twice and then a third time and seemed to relax.

"What now?" asked Nathan.

"We wait." Jacob said. "The Ordnung will, no doubt, already know. I imagine they'll be in contact soon enough. Until then, we will tend to our lives as usual. Just because the world may end does not mean the work will be left undone."

"The Ordnung?" Nathan spoke softly. "The omens only appeared to us, what would they need us for?"

"Because we are now *Coda*." Ansom said. "We are linked by fate, and we are to see this to the end."

Jacob stood, brushed hay from his trousers. "But first," he continued, "we eat. Mary has worked hard this morning, let us not insult her by refusing to partake."

*

The Ordnung's messenger arrived late in the afternoon, bearing a sealed envelope in one hand. In the other hand he held a medallion of silver, slightly larger than a fifty-cent piece. Jacob took both, nodded his thanks and walked to the kitchen. He sat at the table and waited while Mary poured two coffees and sat across from him expectantly. Breaking the seal, Jacob removed the parchment and began to read silently.

"What does it say, Jacob?" Mary asked.

He slid the letter across the table to read for herself. "The other communities have contacted the Ordnung and gave their assent. Tonight, for the first time in seventy-five years, we shall perform the *Riten Van Hoop*. We convene at midnight in Elder Young's barn. I pray that we are successful."

"But why here? Why you?" she asked. "Surely, others have felt the omens."

"Aye, my love. All across the land." Jacob said. "But only we were given a gift." He stood, leaned across the table and kissed Mary upon the forehead. "I must prepare, love."

*

Elder Young greeted each of the six in silence, only allowing them entrance to the barn after each had shown his medallion. Inside stood robed and hooded figures, each holding a guttering torch. They would be the Conclave, overseers of the ritual.

In the center of the large floor was an engraving, deep cut and expertly crafted, of a pyramid made of carved stone blocks, the interior of the capstone contained a representation of a human eye. Each section of pyramid was connected, the etching was one long and unbroken line.

Ancient glyphs surrounded the pyramid, the meanings known to only a handful by design. Jacob felt nausea every time he looked at the runes for longer than a few seconds. The sigils were as polished and free of debris as polished marble; each line and curve shone in the torch light.

A deep voice issued from one of the hooded figures. "It is time. First, place the Medallion of Number."

Cal stepped forward and placed his silver piece upon the circle carved below the foundation of the pyramid, this had been the original starting point when the stone floor was whole and unmarred.

"Second," a different voice this time. "The Medallion of Salvation."

Ansom approached and placed his medallion towards the west and inside of an etched representation of a mother and child, a third of the way up. The silver clinked brightly as it touched stone. The only sound in a room as quiet as a tomb.

A different voice yet again spoke. "Third, the Medallion of Life."

Paul stepped forward and lay his medallion in its corresponding place. The center of the pyramid and equidistant from all sides.

"Fourth." This voice was female and to Jacob's ears vaguely familiar. Goodwife Sarah, perhaps? "The Medallion of Rule."

Nathan glanced to Jacob and stepped forward, his wide eyes peering from below the brim of his hat like chips of ice in sunlight. He slid the medallion into place and hurriedly moved away. Ansom placed a hand upon the boy's shoulder and squeezed.

"Now," came a voice Jacob knew too well. He'd listened to that melodic voice every day since their vows before the Almighty. To say he was surprised was lightly dusting the truth, but he knew that the figures were chosen at random through lottery. It could have been blind chance, but Jacob could almost feel a powerful hand guiding this ritual.

"The Medallion of Cost," his Mary continued, and Jacob stepped forward. The silver medal felt as if it weighed more and more the closer he came to its resting place. The hairs upon his neck stood while gooseflesh danced across his arms. Unbidden, the thought came. *This is what the death of nine billion lives feels like. It's just that easy.*

He took his place and waited. A figure emerged from the shadows of the barn. Hooded as the rest, but carrying a baby girl of no more than a year old; the child was swaddled in a blanket of purest white with only her arms free. She grinned at the men who stood before her with an innocence that was heartbreaking. "Owner of the gift, step forward." The figure holding the child said. "Place your gift into the child's hand and the Medallion of Reckoning into the final space."

The child took the marble into her hands and cooed softly. Thomas leaned forward and placed a kiss upon her forehead. She giggled and grasped at his beard. "Will you witness as well, *Kado*?" The figure asked.

"I will." Thomas replied and turned, nodding to each of those that had made up his Coda. Jacob gave a solemn bow of his head and placed a hand upon his heart. Thomas stood in the capstone and placed his medal into the center of the eye.

The child was held above the Medallion of Number, within seconds the marble slipped from her grasp to land upon the medals' edge. Careening away, it began to skitter down the carved rut towards the pyramid's foundation. The marble hissed along its path, catching subtly rounded corners and picking up speed upon the imperfections of sacred stone.

Jacob watched, not the path, but Thomas. He watched as tendrils of light the color of summertime grass coiled around Thomas's legs and wove their way upwards. They encircled his arms and caressed his broad chest. The light found his eyes, filled them as he stiffened; his mouth was a silent scream and his body was as unmoving as stone.

Thomas felt the pain of one man who had lost everything. His material wealth remained, reputation and future were still whole. This man cared not for those things. No. What he loved most was the family that was taken from him in fire and hate. Wrong place, wrong time. They'd waited for him as he worked; waited for an hour or more. Long enough for the explosive to detonate. Casualties in a battle that had nothing to do with them. Over time the grief rooted deep. Madness and regret had taken hold, grew insidious and vile inside him and twisted his views. He'd burn them all, he'd use every means at his disposal to turn the world to ashes.

The marble danced across the Medallion of Life and kicked it from its place. Farther it rolled, through the lines and ridges of carved rock and sigils of an older time. It skated across the Medallion of Salvation as if it was as insubstantial as a fever dream.

He ignored the pleas for forgiveness and understanding that came from the churches. He spat upon those who had sided with either side of the conflict and turned a blind eye to those who'd suffered as he had. He was single minded, obsessed. And beginning to go mad. He made deals with criminals, who made deals with criminals who made deals with governments. He funneled his wealth into weapons of mass destruction, cheap on the Eastern Blocs if you knew who to know. He bought a shipping container full of VTX gas for less than what his first car had cost him.

Thomas juddered and twitched, blood seeping from his ears and nostrils. Jacob wanted to look away, found he could not. The marble popped and sizzled down its track. A curve and the glass ball struck the Medallion of Rule.

The man was a warlord now. Thousands of victims at his feet as the deadly agents he bought and stole were released into cities. Governments wanted his head, insurgents clamored for his leadership. He allied with one nation, the wrong nation. He showed them formula and cache, the fires of Hell held in glass and floating fogs that would strip the flesh from man as he screamed. They welcomed him, praised him and then they executed him and strung his body for all to see.
And then they used the gifts he had brought them to impose their version of salvation.

The marble skipped once across the lines carved deep and bounded into the Medallion of Cost. Thomas was gurgling now. Small wet sounds that issued from deep within.

Billions dead. The Oceans no longer teemed with anything but sludge and decay. Nothing flew or swam. Nothing walked. Nothing would, ever again. The Earth was a dead world now, so decayed and poisoned that life and death would both flee from its sickly visage.

The marble was losing momentum as it approached the Medallion of Reckoning and Jacob found himself silently urging it onwards. He glanced to those around him, surprised to see the robed figures had retreated into the shadows where they were barely visible. The rest of his Coda stood silent and expecting, barely breathing as they watched the fate of the world play out. He prayed for Thomas, for the world.

A voice reached Thomas from across the wastelands. **Would you damn your soul for those you've never met?**

"Yes." He replied.

Would you damn her soul? Would you pay that price for those who'd rather piss upon your grave as lend you a helping hand?

"It's an entire world." Thomas said. "Nine billion lives. What is her soul compared to that?"

Eternal torment. A billion billion years of agony waiting for her in the darkness?

"Damnation is a small price to pay." Thomas said.

The voice was silent as a fetid wind danced across a blasted and corrupted landscape.

What if she were returned to you? Alive, whole and healthy. No one need know but you. You'd have years together before the end. What then, Kado?

Thomas was silent for a long, long time. "No." Thomas said. "I'd no longer be the man she loved. Your offer is refused."

The marble came to rest upon the medallion that lay in the center of the eye. A bright white light radiated outward from the center of the marble to fill the room in a blinding glare. The pressure of a thousand thousand sighs blew through the air and cleansed each figure it touched of doubt, worry, and fear. The *Kado*, the offering, had been accepted and the world would continue to turn on its axis. Thomas lay crumpled upon the ground, unmoving.

The Coda came for him, Jacob getting there first and holding

Thomas's head in his lap. The others spoke softly, murmuring softly of thanks and appreciation before retreating exhausted into the night.

The silent robed figures emerged from the shadows to file by, each touching the brow of the Kado. As the last neared the door of the barn, she turned and fixed her gaze upon Jacob. As he watched, she placed a hand upon her heart and tapped twice. Jacob rose shaking fingers to his lips, kissed and placed his hand across his heart. Mary disappeared into the night.

*

Epilogue:

Victor was running late again. Maria and the kids were waiting near the elevators for him and he'd been sidetracked. This vacation to Hong Kong hadn't really worked out well for him or his family. Business was once more taking over and he'd spent most of his time on the phone or computer. More now than he had back at the office, at any rate. Maria was beginning to get angry at his lack of attention. And the kids, well...

Victor wasn't sure when the last time he'd told the kids he'd loved them. He needed to change that, needed to—

The cell phone beeped again, demanding his attention. He could see them, waiting impatiently while Maria stared daggers of frustration. "Hon," he called out. "Go on down to the little coffee shop and wait for me. I just need to take this last call."

He watched them until the doors closed. Oh yeah, Victor thought. She is *pissed*. He turned heading back towards the hotel room when a man seemed to appear from nowhere and place his hand upon Victor's shoulder stopping him in his tracks. Victor felt small electric tingles radiate from the man's hand, up his neck, and across his scalp. He couldn't seem to focus on anything but the touch and the stranger's eyes. Leaning forward, the odd figure placed his mouth next to Victor's ear. Victor could feel the soft bristles of the man's beard tickle his neck.

"Business can wait, my friend. This is all fleeting, only love will remain."

And then he was gone. Victor stood alone in the hotel hallway, slightly disoriented. Had the man really been there? Already, the memory was fading. The phone rang again and Victor powered the phone down. "Business can wait." he said and made his way to the elevator.

~END~

The Acolyte
By Dan Gainor

Caleb moved slowly through the trees and dense brush. He had been hunting since he was a young buwe. This was the first time he ever hunted a man. He was covered in the simple green uniform and carried a Suisse-made AK-57. Caleb moved with purpose, trying to stay quiet and scan for threats.

Jeremiah was ahead and off to the right. He stepped with confidence and never even looked down. He preferred to work close. His left hand held a Harrisburg .45-caliber pistol, or Burger for short. The right held a more precise weapon – an Israeli Masada V-21. It shot the same .45-caliber shells, but there the similarity ended. The Burger was a clunky weapon. It could kill, sure, but it wasn't reliable enough for this kind of work. The Feld craftsmen were far inferior to the other major powers.

Jeremiah didn't want to kill their target—at least not right away. They had been tracking him since outside of old Philadelphia. The Masada was a thing of beauty, made of ceramic and a steel alloy beyond even the capabilities of top Suisse armorers. In the hands of the right shooter, it would never miss.

Caleb's training deacon had told him time and again to trust his gut, and this day that advice saved his life. When he felt eyes on him he stepped slightly to the left, behind a thick oak, right before the first bullet whizzed by, right where he had been standing. The next two slammed into the tree sending splinters flying right by Caleb's face. He raised the rifle and tried to estimate where the shots had come from.

The hunters had become the hunted, and the acolyte knew real fear for the first time in his life.

Another shot rang out, a pistol this time. Then Jeremiah's voice muttered "Damn," quietly under his breath.

"You can come out. It's safe."

Caleb walked over and Jeremiah was already searching the shooter's body. On the surface, he looked like one of the Folk, but not on closer inspection. Yes, the clothes may have been homespun—he got that right—but the shoes were too nice. Amish cobblers did a good job; their shoes were simple, practical. Yet these were just too fancy. Too Englisch.

The acolyte turned to his deacon, "Suisse?"

Jeremiah only nodded. He didn't have the heart to tell Caleb that the kill shot had saved his life.

To Hades with the mission. He was responsible for the acolyte. And this one would live... at least for now.

*

The first shots were close – less than a mile away. They could have been hunters. They certainly came from a long gun and Amish men certainly liked to hunt. It was the second gun that sent fear up Hannah's spine. That was a pistol. No hunter used a pistol.

That meant only one of the two things – both potentially bad. The first was raiders. The attacks weren't as often as in the dark times. They still happened. The empty spot in her bed was a constant reminder. What was left of Pittsburgh was too close to Smithton and the remains of the Englisch still lived there.

The other side of the coin were The Feld—the fighters who defended the Amish against threats. Many were good. A few were almost as bad as the raiders, preying on farmers, taking what they wanted. She absentmindedly pulled her blouse closer. Sometimes they took anything they wanted.

She raced around the farm to find her kinder as quietly as she could. She had all four with her and was heading inside when the riders approached. They were well-fed, dressed in dark green and carrying a body slung over a pack horse. The one in the lead had a blank expression as he scanned constantly for threats. The younger one smiled unconvincingly.

The older man—a deacon she guessed—got off his horse and stepped toward them. Hannah held her oldest daughter close, protectively. Rebecca was 15 and looked more woman than girl. When he approached, the deacon removed his hat, which in itself marked him as someone not of the Folk. It wasn't wide-brimmed like the Ordnung mandated. It was a baseball cap style, though that game was rarely played anymore. He wiped his brow with his sleeve, and his overall demeanor seemed.

"I'm Deacon Jeremiah, this is my acolyte, Caleb. We need a place to wash up, a nice bed and a home-cooked meal." He looked from the girl to her mamm. "That's all we want."

Hannah relaxed a bit.

Her son, Noah, spoke up, pulling out of his mamm's embrace before she could silence him. "Is that a real pistol?" He asked, pointing at the Burger at Jeremiah's belt.

The deacon started to reach for the gun to show the buwe but paused, as he saw the look of fear on Hannah's face. "Perhaps when you're older."

Hannah smiled weakly. The Rumsfeld, she didn't dare speak the nickname... they hadn't come for her family.

*

Levi could barely hide his excitement, pacing rapidly around the farmhaus under the watchful eye of his mamm. The other kinder had never seen him like this. Levi Kurtz was a proper young Amish buwe.
He had just turned 16. Mamm was allowing him and a few other youngies to attend a party in Harrisburg as part of rumschpringe. It was going to be the first time any of them had been away from home without adults.

Rumschpringe had remained part of Amish culture even after The

Hack. There were lots of Amish in this part of Pennsylvania and the farms were mostly safe enough for youngies to be normal teens for a bit. They could stay on main roads through Lancaster and on to Harrisburg without any trouble. Those areas were well-patrolled by police. Raiders seldom moved this far into Pennsylvania from the wild lands of the cities to the east.

The other three friends arrived by bicycle. The fair-haired Mary was the first to arrive – wearing a homespun dress in a blue plaid. Still conservative but not the typical solid color that marked the Amish. She was the only girl in the group and the prettiest one in her class. They treated her like a sister. Mamm wanted her to marry one of them, preferably the stable Levi, but Mary knew it wouldn't happen.

Next came Samuel, strong as an ox only shy with those outside his circle of friends. He had known Levi since they were bobbeli and they were closer than bruders they resembled. Both had auburn hair and brown eyes and were solidly built from a lifetime of farm work. Their clothes hadn't changed much—they lacked Mary's skill with a needle.

Alex was the last to arrive. He still wore his plain homespun clothes like the other buwes. There the resemblances ended. Alex had been a foundling. Daed had rescued the young buwe from one of the refugee caravans that had fallen victim to the Hack—those madmen and women had butchered his caravan. His true mamm had hid the bobbeli beneath some clothes with his name hastily scribbled on a piece of paper. The attackers only wanted food and victims.

Alex's parents had been Sikhs who had fled New York during the collapse. They were trying to reach Amish country like so many others.

There was a time when his looks and Englisch name would have marked Alex as an outsider. No more. Tens of thousands had flocked to the Amish communities, first in the U.S. and then in Europe and South America. The rampant intrusion of technology into lives, bodies and, eventually brains was more than many could take.

They rebelled and joined the Amish and Mennonite communities who welcomed them with open arms. A simpler life without internet and

Borgtech beckoned many.

Rumschpringe was supposed to be a time of choosing to stay or leave. All four teens knew they would stay; Alex more than the others. He loved his family. The community was an island of sanity in a world gone mad.

The sound of vehicles changed everything.

*

The dinner table was tense. Hannah prepared a large meal, hoping to keep the Feld happy and distracted. Chicken, potatoes, corn, tomatoes and more filled plates and bowls.

The acolyte sat across from Rebecca and his face reddened every time she looked back at him. He wasn't much older than her, as he'd joined the Feld at the time of rumschpringe when he was 16. This was his first real mission.

Across the table, Noah continued to stare at the deacon and his gun. "Tell us what it's like fighting the bad men." His mamm's repeated instructions to shush held no sway.

"It's a lot of travel," Jeremiah answered. "I've been with the Feld since the early days, seen all the city ruins along the eastern seaboard. Even crossed the Atlantic, seen the Amish colonies in France and Spain. Of course, that was during the hot war with the Suissies. Now, it's pretty cold, for the most part, though there are still skirmishes here and there, enough danger that you should be wise to stick close to home.

"Now, enough stories. I have to speak with your mamm. Caleb, there's still plenty of light, go chop some wood." He nodded to the empty place at the head of the table. The acolyte left, followed closely the Rebecca.

Jeremiah trailed Hannah into the sewing room and he closed the door.

Hannah caught her breath. "My mann Daniel…"

"Don't lie. I mean you no harm. The farm is in too much disrepair for there to be a mann here."

She stared at the floor, unable to speak.

"Raiders?" Jeremiah asked.

She nodded yes.

"I'm sorry that we weren't here to protect you. That is why we're here. To stop what they are doing up in Pittsburgh. And I need your help."

"How can I..."

"There must be one in the community who trades with the Englisch. It happens everywhere. They have things we need—tools, metals and such. I need his help."

She didn't hesitate. "Moses, two farms over, he takes his wagon there once a week and trades food for... things."

Jeremiah grabbed her hand gently and placed several silver pieces in it.

"Och, I can't," Hannah said.

"It will help make up for our visit, and it will cover for things when your buwe joins up."

"Joins?!? He's too young, he's only 10." Her face turned white with fear.

"It won't matter. He'll join. I've seen that look before and I'm never wrong. Take this." He gave her his card that only said Deacon Jeremiah Erb. "Hand him this when the time comes. If I'm still alive, I'll try to see that he gets something other than combat. Maybe his blood will cool a bit with desk duty."

Hannah squeezed his hand. "Bless you."

*

Levi's mamm Elizabeth was a strong woman. As she looked about the kitchen, tears started to flow. It was a simple Amish kitchen, with plenty of food. The basement and spring house held much more. That didn't even account for the stock. "If we just give the Englisch what they want..." Daed was off to town selling some produce. Levi realized quickly that made him head of the haus.

"No." He motioned his mamm to the basement. "Take Becky and Jacob."

She saw him reach for the shotgun he used to hunt. "You can't. We don't. We're Amish."

"Rumschpringe started today. Today, we can act Englisch if we want to. If they want to rob and butcher us, they'll find out the Amish are done being victims." He tossed daed's shotgun to Alexa who was the better shot. Mary grabbed a butcher knife from the kitchen. Samuel picked the poker from the fireplace. There was a look of determination on their faces. They were youngies no more.

"Remember, we don't fight them if they will just leave." Levi placed himself to the left of the front door and took aim.

The raiders came in an SUV and a panel van. They were really set on taking as much loot as they could.

Spotter started barking up a storm, like he did anytime strangers arrived. A gunshot silenced his alarm. Spotter had been Levi's dog since he was 7.

Levi cocked the shotgun. There was no turning back now. Blood had been shed.

Alex was the first to fire. He saw another man ready to kill one of the cows. He knew what raiders could do. He wasn't going to let it happen a second time.

A pair of raiders kicked in the front door and were met by both barrels of Levi's shotgun.

The remaining raiders never made it back to their vehicles.

The Feld had been born.

*

Abram had insisted that the two Feld spend a day loading and unloading the wagon, so they knew what he had and where, especially how to access the secret compartments. Jeremiah tried to be understanding. Abram was scared. For once, not scared of the Feld.

He was scared of the Englisch.

Those weren't raiders. There were still a few thousand or maybe many more in the city, an established community with guards and leaders. They were starving and deadly. Some of the hacked roamed the ruins… and they would eat anything or anyone!

The only thing that kept them all in Pittsburgh was the Feld. A full regiment had crushed the city defenders several years before. The residents remembered.

Abram's farm was on an old golf course west of what used to be Smithton, southeast of the big city. The wagon ride would take at least three days. The guns and their essential gear went into one of the many secret hideaways in the covered wagon. All three men carried Bowie knives, standard for farmers these days. Wild dogs were one of the many relics of civilization that continued to threaten a man alone.

Moses filled them in on the dynamics of the city as they traveled. "Just tell them you are cousins who lost your homes to raiders. I'm taking you in until you can save up enough for a new farm. They don't really care about us. They just want the food we bring."

Jeremiah rode up front next to Moses. Caleb sat on the back of the wagon, keeping look out there. The wagon was large and solidly built. It took four oxen just to pull its heavy load—of corn and flour, milk and cheese. The wagon travelled slowly down what had once been back roads. The major highways were too expensive to maintain. Amish kept the secondary roads clear for travel.

They passed so many rotted husks of autos that they were beyond counting. Most of the newer homes had either been torn down for salvage or burned in the madness of the Hack. The closer they came to Pittsburgh, the more desolate it became.

The road narrowed to a poorly maintained path between young trees and bushes. Mankind's mark was being erased by nature, slowly but surely.

Yet, not so with Pittsburgh. The towers of the big city showed in the distance, even though many had been destroyed in the violence that followed the collapse of the world's tech powers. Jeremiah knew if reports were true, he was going up against the Suissies again. They fought like maniacs. The Folk outnumbered them these days many times over, but the Suisse Republic now covered the mountainous areas from what used to be France through Italy, Switzerland, Germany and Austria.

He remembered the battles in Europe. The Folk controlled most everything else there now. Amish farmers plowed the arable lands of Europe. Feld companies guarded the borders with the Suisse. South America, Australia and North America were also dominated by the Folk. Asia had devolved in roving warlords. Israel controlled the Middle East and influenced the politics of the rest of Africa.

The fighting with the Suisse had been a stalemate. They had far-better weapons, but few troops and limited supplies in their mountain hideaways where food was always a problem. The Feld had large numbers of poorly armed troops. And only a few expensive weapons either captured from the Suisse or bought from Israel.

The Amish and Suisse were natural enemies. The old ways vs. the new. Israel tried to keep the peace with both and supplied them, discreetly. It had enough trouble feeding and keeping the peace with the restive Muslim populations. It didn't want another war.

If reports were correct about Pittsburgh, the Suisse were about to strike at the heart of the Amish world—the capital of Harrisburg.

It was up to Jeremiah to learn the truth, and if an attack were imminent, find a way to stop it.

*

Levi and his friends took the guns and their story to Harrisburg to meet with the council of bishops. The massive influx of Englisch into the community had forced some changes on the independent Amish districts. They had appointed a council of bishops to reconcile some of the disparate teachings.

Most Amish districts wanted to be staunchly independent. The Englisch inside and out had changed that. Amish districts now worked together for survival.

Four armed Amish youngies changed things more than any who had gone before them.

Levi walked solemnly before the council and told the shocked bishops what had taken place. How four Amish had killed six raiders before they could devastate another Amish farm. Before they could rape and kill more Amish women. He then presented his plan. And told them in no uncertain terms that he and his friends were committed to the idea. Rumschpringe had put them on their path of gelassenheit—the Amish belief of doing for the community, not for themselves.

Levi, Samuel, Mary, and Alex were forming a military unit to defend the peaceful Amish. They would respect Amish traditions and beliefs and be non-violent when possible. But they would be the sword of the community, to defend homes or strike at the heart of attackers.

And they were doing it whether the council approved or not.

The bishops were tired of Amish funerals. The strains were felt throughout the Folk that perhaps the peaceful people needed to hammer plowshares into swords.

Levi's plan gave them an out. The bishops approved the Feld. It was a seemingly non-military term, meaning they were the Amish who would take to the field. The bishops knew the term had military usage and had for hundreds of years. Secretly some had been contemplating something similar.

The story of Amish who would fight traveled through the Folk like lightning. Die Botschaft, the Amish newspaper, treated the youngie like heroes. Rumschpringe turned into a time of choosing, not to stay in the community or leave, but to farm or join the Feld. There was nowhere else to go now. It became a choosing of the traditional Amish path or joining the military arm.

First hundreds, then thousands, flocked to the Feld. Englisch mocked the term, combining it with rumschpringe to nickname the group after a former United States Secretary of Defense—the *Rumsfeld*.
The nickname stuck. Only, as the Feld grew in power, few dared call them that. Except themselves.

*

Armed guards greeted the wagon as it moved close to campus, the center of activity in fallen Pittsburgh. By the look on Moses's face, that was new. He tried to play it cool.

Wagon arrivals were always an occasion. There were other Amish who came in from the outer ring of the city. There was always a chance for the lucky to trade goods for food. Steel, tin, and copper were once in the city in abundance. It had been mined for years and each day grew more difficult.

The food from old stores had long run out. There wasn't enough open land in parks and sports fields to feed the city.

Pittsburgh was dying slowly. Yet, it didn't look it.

The city had a vibrancy to it, an organization that smelled Suisse to Jeremiah. The guards were scarecrow thin and dressed in rags, but the guns they carried looked new. The arms weren't Suisse; they were something he hadn't seen before and that was scary in itself. Maybe Arab or South African. How did they get here? And in enough numbers that ordinary street thugs had them.

Jeremiah kept focus on the task as they came to the market or "Frick" as the locals called it. There was a large, low building still standing with numerous stalls placed around it. What was left of a fountain sat in the center before the steps. And three metal doors marked the main entrance. They could just make out the word "Frick" on the building. That meant all of this was part of the old university—back when America had such things. Amish schooling ended at high school and most never finished that. The Feld had a small technical college, which was why the Amish were so far behind the Suisse and Israelis.

Jeremiah was thankful there were no other Folk nearby. Just local craftsmen selling pathetic homegrowns, poorly made pottery, and some things scavengers had found—everything from knives to poorly preserved magazines.

"Put your wagon over by that wall," ordered the guard who appeared to be in charge. He and his bully buwes quickly chased away onlookers. "This isn't for you, this is for the boss," he told them

It was getting to be twilight and the guard told them they could deal in the morning. "Don't go far or ya might get chopped," said the man, laughing.

Caleb waited until they had left and started to reach for the secret compartment with the pistols. Jeremiah put a hand on his shoulder and shook his head. "If they find us far away from the wagon, maybe we can get away with a tourist story or maybe we just get beat up. If they find us with guns, they'll kill us for sure. And they'll take their time about it."

He patted Moses on the back and they moved into the crowd trying to gawk at least a little.

Caleb had no problem with that. The building they called the Cathedral of Learning stood several blocks away. Even damaged from the fighting or the fires, it dominated the sky. Caleb had never seen a building over six floors. Few people outside the cities had.

*

Jeremiah was one of the few Feld to have seen a city before the fall. Thirty years later, he was one of the oldest deacons out on duty. All the others had either retired to farms or moved into administrative roles with the Feld.

The collapse was still too real for Jeremiah. He'd witnessed it in a way he had never told another soul about.

Some children get parties and toys for their birthdays. Jeremiah got an apocalypse.

The family had lived in a fancy high-rise on the 75th floor of the city's first arcology—The Manhattan Masterpiece. Dad worked for what had been a Wall Street firm whose HQ was now one of the prime tenants.

The party was really just the four of them, mom and dad and sister Eileen.

Dad had recently upgraded to the Michelangelo VVs, the latest in brain-enhancement tech. They cost more than a home for most Americans. He needed it for work and splurged getting a second set for his wife.

It was all about the social status.

Only, the Jupiter Hacker Collective resented the new implants. None of them could afford them, so they devoted every waking hour to hacking them to teach others a lesson.

Daaavil-Proton was the best of the best in Jupiter and he found a way in. Only he refused to tell the others—eager to claim sole credit. He had hardly slept for two weeks, devoting all of his time to cracking the new Borgtech.

When he found his way in, he thought he was lowering the users' moral inhibitions. He envisioned some of the nation's most important people rutting right in the middle of the street. It wasn't harmless, but it was so embarrassing he thought he'd escape prosecution.

DP, as his friends called him, was right about the hack. Only he was wrong about what he changed. He tapped into anger, not lust. A few thousand of the rich and famous were instantly and deadly furious. That would have been bad enough. Except the software was backwards compatible. That flooded the entire network.

More than 1 billion people had some sort of brain-enhancement. Nearly the entire world was soon flooded with humans turned mad killers. Only Israel and Switzerland were exempt. Israel was denied Borgtech as part of the global boycott against the struggling Jewish state.

Meanwhile, a Suisse scientist noticed The Hack in time and officials shut down the network in that isolated nation. The mountains helped keep out the signals.

The two nations were rapidly surrounded by raving violent lunatics.

For Israel, this was nothing new, but the Suisse hadn't been on a war footing in hundreds of years. It took time to adjust.

Jeremiah saw all of it from the eyes of a terrified 8-year-old buwe. He went to open the big box and his mom smacked him with a lamp, screaming like a monster from a holo-flick. Blood poured into his eyes as he watched his father pounce on Eileen, stabbing her repeatedly with scissors. Then the parents went at each other, kicking, punching and biting. Dad won quickly. He smashed his wife's head into the heavy glass window. Blood and brains slid down to the floor.

Jeremiah did the only thing he could do, he pretended to be dead. He didn't dare move or even breathe. Dad soon raced out of the apartment screaming at the top of his lungs.

Jeremiah crawled to the door and closed it quietly.

Then he passed out.

*

Caleb walked wide-eyed through the Frick market. Harrisburg had markets, though it didn't allow flesh or drugs. In Pittsburg, everything was for sale—prices and lives were cheap.

One blonde turned to face him and opened her robe. She was naked and scrawny underneath. The scene still awakened lust in the young man. He stumbled away when he saw the woman pick up a bobbeli and hold it to her breast, robe still open.

He turned to Jeremiah, "Can't we do anything to help them?"

The deacon shook his head slowly no.

"But not even the kinder?"

"You want a real war, start stealing bobbeli from the Englisch. They love their kinder, just as we do."

Caleb grew quiet as they walked east. A large barricade blocked their path. An ugly concrete building was 100 yards behind the well-guarded barricade.

Jeremiah turned away, taking the acolyte's arm. "Did you notice? They have some large lights, only they are pointed up, not at the ground."

"What does that mean?"

"It means you are going back to the wagon and I'm going to find out."

"You can't …" Caleb said to empty air. The deacon was already gone.

He wandered back to the wagon, steering clear of the flesher and her bobbeli. It was too much to take.

*

Jeremiah found an easy spot to slip through a hole in the fence. There were several guards, though they didn't appear to be guarding much. He carefully worked his way to the concrete building.

Climbing still bothered the deacon more than he'd ever let on. He had done too much of it descending for the heights of the arcology fleeing New York. The escape that his young mind thought would take hours instead took months.

It hardened the buwe into the man he became. Stealth became a life skill. Without it, he would have died. Few made it out of the big cities. The hacked took their toll and desperation and hunger took most of the rest.

Jeremiah walked by night and burrowed into the ground by day like a mole. He was starving by the time he hit Pennsylvania. He saw a horse and buggy just like in the vids and followed it. Knocking sheepishly on the door, the buwe prayed for help.

Daed had opened the door. He was in his 50s at that point in his life, long past raising a young buwe. He took one look at the starving 10-year-old and said without hesitation, "You'll be staying with us now."

They nursed him back to his strength and Jeremiah worked like a demon to pay them. The farm prospered. Only the buwe never truly fit in.

News came of the Feld when Jeremiah was 14. Daed took him aside and said matter of factly, "They'll be needing strong young ones like you." Jeremiah merely nodded, unable to thank the man who'd welcomed him as a son and so readily let him go.

The pair were inseparable for the next two years. Daed taught Jeremiah every trick of hunting, fishing and tracking he had learned in 50 years. He filled in the gaps of what the buwe had learned out of fear and necessity.

Climbing was one of the few things daed couldn't improve on. Climbing down from the top floor of a darkened, powerless, 75-floor building and escaping the nightmare of New York had taught Jeremiah more about climbing manmade structures than he'd ever need to know. The climb up the few stories to the top of this new concrete construct took little time. Jeremiah was relieved to see no guards on the roof. He kept low and surveyed the area. There were more lights around the edge, once more aiming up.

Only these weren't handmade or scavenged. These were real and the best Suisse tech. The roof was dotted with several new anchor fittings. Jeremiah had seen the like in France. He had his answer. They were for a Suisse blimp.

He had the answer alright. The Suisse were supplying the Englisch in Pittsburgh and maybe every city in old America. They had figured out a way to get behind the Amish lines and had to be stopped hard or thousands of Amish would die as a result.

Jeremiah felt the approaching guard more than heard him. He grabbed the climbing rope and launched himself off the side. He kept the road tight and almost ran down the side of the building.

They'd find the rope later. That couldn't be helped. He had to get back.

*

The dean's security moved fast through the Frick. If there was spying going on, it had to be the Amish. Yet two guard outposts claimed no one had returned since early evening.

The guards surrounded the wagon and the biggest of the bunch screamed, "Get up!"

Caleb and Moses stumbled to their feet. It was still dark. They feared Jeremiah had been caught. "Where's the other one?" roared the dean. When neither man answered, he shouted, "Tie them up, we'll roast them for the hacked to enjoy. Teach them to spy."

There was a rustling from inside the wagon. The guards aimed their guns and Jeremiah poked his head out. "How's a man to get sleep around here?"

Two of the guards grabbed him by the arms and pulled him from the wagon. A small bottle fell from his pocket. Another guard picked it up, sniffed it, and laughed. He handed it to the dean. "I thought these pig sloppers didn't drink."

The dean sniffed it and looked at Jeremiah. "Well?"

"I never had it before, I just had to try it. Wow, does my head hurt."

"You weren't near Barco?"

"What's a Barcooo?" Jeremiah began to cough like he was sick, leaned over and surreptitiously stuck his finger down his throat. The bile of cheap market food and liquor came up quickly.

The dean looked at him. "That'll teach ya to drink too much licker," he said, satisfied. He turned to Moses. "The wagon load is good. I need more, lots more. And soon. Maybe three weeks."

Moses didn't have to play scared. He was terrified by everything now. "I, I, ca, ca, can't. The Feld. They'd know."

The dean held out a handful of shiny new gold coins. "I can pay, top dollar."

Jeremiah stood up, stumbling a bit. Then he walked right up to the dean. And reached out his hand. "I'll do it." He took one of the gold and stared at it.

The gold piece was marked with the Suisse cross on one side and the image of a mountain on the other. It said "100 Suisse francs." Jeremiah just stood there and stared at it.

The gold piece felt powerful in his hand. "I've never even seen gold before. Sure ain't held it."

"I can give ya these and more if'n ya come back with 10 wagons or more in three week's time."

Now Caleb stepped forward, playing his part well. "I'm in."

"I'll give ya 10 now and 10 later," the dean said.

Jeremiah shook his head. "I don't need 10 now. But the Feld will hang us if they catch us. Five is enough to buy what we need. So five now and 20 later."

He looked over at Caleb. "Twenty-five gold will set us both up with farms and a pair of pretty young wives to take care of us."

The dean smiled and counted out five gold pieces. "We'll find ya, if you don't come back."

"If I don't come back for 20 gold, it's because I'm killt."

*

It took them two-and-a-half days back with an empty wagon just back to Moses' farm. Jeremiah went directly to the barn where he had hidden an Israeli radio, which was both encrypted and allegedly undetectable, even by the Suisse.

When Caleb saw it, he suddenly realized the importance of their mission. Just that one radio cost enough to fund a company of Feld for a year or more.

Jeremiah radioed in the need for troops and wagons filled with food. The Feld had an easy way into the city. All they had to do was look like they were working for the man called the dean.

The farm became a rallying point for Feld. The relative peace in the area meant few Feld were actually available. The first there procured wagons and food, adding a false front to store weapons. Twenty Feld were going in to take out the blimp. The rest would sweep in from the river.

Caleb tried asking about the civilians in Pittsburgh and what would happen to them. The only response he got back was cold and emotionless, "What will happen to our people if the Englisch invade with Suisse weapons?" It was the math of war. And war had been declared.

A week after the call, more than a company of Feld arrived in full combat gear. Most carried rifles, but the men driving the wagons were given Israeli TT40s, nicknamed TatTat because of their ability to spray bullets on target without recoil making them miss.

Hidden in each wagon was a rocket, to be used only against the blimp. Rockets were advanced for the Feld. Nine of them were homemade in a special Harrisburg arms facility. The tenth was the one Jeremiah carried in his wagon. That was Suisse made, captured five years back during fighting in France. If it worked, it would be a fitting present for the invaders.

The troops moved out to the west of the wagon train. A driver and a guard manned each of the wagons. A few of the men carried bows for the wild dogs. This much food was bound to attract attention.

The wagons were filled with all sorts of food—produce, meat, cheese—jars and jars of food ready for winter. Unconsciously, Caleb wondered if it could be returned. This much food probably left the locals with little to fall back on.

It was necessary. He hoped.

*

The timing was crucial. They guessed the dean wanted them there before the dark of the moon for a reason—that would be an ideal time for the blimp to land safely.

They traveled deliberately, staying to the east of one of Pittsburgh's great rivers, the Monongahela. This route would also keep them from having to cross the Allegheny, which would have been arduous, for few of the bridges survived. Some had been destroyed in the conflict, others were wrecked either by the Feld or the residents for mutual protection.

Nothing dared mess with the wagons. Even dogs sensed more threat than was worth the effort. The Feld traveled mostly in silence, always listening, always on guard. The Amish weren't always so serious, but this was serious business. Were the cover story true, all 20 of the men would be committing a most heinous crime.

The Feld didn't forgive.

The company of Feld moved off to the west, on the other side of the river. They had already dispatched two enemy scouts. So far they hadn't been discovered.

Every step closer to the city made that more likely.

*

Four wide-eyed guards stopped them as they approached the city. From the way they drooled, Caleb guessed they had never imagined this much food. Here it was for the taking and they were too scared of the dean to grab even a mouthful.

It was late in the day and the market was quiet.

The crowd was armed better than the last time they had been in the city. Guards escorted them to the Frick and they lined up the wagons and corralled the horses.

It was getting dark and most of the Feld were bedding down. Then they heard a hum. It started low and grew louder. Then came a hammering sound.

Jeremiah moved toward the wagon as another of the Feld began to wake up the others discreetly. The deacon reached into the wagon like he was getting some supplies, as he watched the crowd. Only, the armed natives didn't react. Many of them were also bedding down, or joining each other in sin, heedless of who watched them.

Jeremiah wiped his brow and took a careful look at the Barco. There were no lights, no crowds, nothing. This wasn't the Suisse. This was something else. Another thing to worry about. He was thankful for the moonless night.

Once more he sneaked out into the dangerous city.

*

Following the sound was harder than it should've been. Jeremiah worked mostly in the countryside. Sound waves didn't bounce off of buildings and ruins there.

The hunt for the mysterious goings on took some time. Oddly, it wasn't the sound that helped most, it was the smell. Jeremiah smelled a coal fire, and tracked its source.

The building was long and low, made of brick. It had once been a warehouse and then a high-priced condominium from the look of things. Now it had gone back to its industrial roots. Coal smoke poured out of two chimneys, and noise filled the street.

Jeremiah knew that no one could hear him. He feared he would be discovered because he couldn't hear them either. He saw a coal pile outside and rubbed his face and hands in coal dust for concealment. He would look the part of a workman, at least. That would have to be cleaned off later before returning to the wagons.

The door was guarded. The windows were wide open and unattended. He slipped through one and landed between a row of long, rough-hewn boxes. They were unlabeled, but the lid wasn't on tight. He lifted it and nearly fell over from shock. The box held three newly made rifles, coated in grease. From their design, he guessed they were single shot. That still made them dangerous.

Smaller boxes held pistols. They matched the unique design the guards carried outside. A peek around the corner and Jeremiah learned the secret.

The guns were being made right here in Pittsburgh. Enough guns for a couple regiments of troops. Enough guns to start a second front in the war with the Suisse and unite the remaining Englisch in the cities.

Jeremiah knew a dirty secret. There weren't that many Feld troops in old America. They were mostly in Europe or in the wilds of South America. The Feld were about to be outnumbered and outgunned right near their own capital.

He didn't wait around. He slipped out and saw another building several hundred yards behind this factory and it looked like it had workers as well. He guessed it could be an ammunition factory.

He had no way of telling the rest of the Feld what awaited them in the city. Their mission objective had been to destroy the blimp. Now that airship was the least of their worries.

*

Jeremiah told the others what he'd found. If the attack failed, they'd have to get back and sound the alarm. They'd have to evacuate every farm for miles to prevent a slaughter. The Feld would be fighting a delaying action against a growing army while they pulled forces back across the ocean. And that would take months.

The Suisse weren't stupid.

The dean sent one of his guards to thank Jeremiah and tell him he and Caleb would have to wait to be paid. Jeremiah asked why the delay. The guard told him the food was for "special guests."

Blimps mostly held cargo and small crews, but if they needed 10 wagons of food, it must have carried troops, not cargo. *The Suisse were invading!*
Jeremiah's mind went wild with the thought. Thousands of armed Englisch led by competent leaders with troops armed with advanced weapons. It was a war the Feld could easily lose.

He sat down to think and to conserve his strength. The next few hours might determine the future for Amish everywhere.

Waiting was hard on some of the men. Especially Caleb. He had too much fear and adrenalin. The deacon assigned his acolyte to cook for the others and that distracted him.

The day passed slowly. When night fell, the Frick woke up. A lot.

This was different than how the locals had acted before. They were excited, eager. Many began to celebrate. There was dancing and singing and lots and lots of drinking. No matter how starved they were for food, somehow they found ways to make alcohol.

By 9 p.m., the crowd was whipped into a frenzy. Even the guards were drinking. There was a distant hum, almost impossible to hear over the crowd. It grew louder and one of the lights on the roof of Barco went on, turning the night sky to daylight.

Jeremiah nodded and the Feld dispatched the guards, with two of their number taking their place.

"We are too far away. I have an idea. Put the rockets and TatTats in the back of two of the wagons. We'll go among the people and give out food like it's part of the celebration. When it gets close, we fire the rockets at the blimp and open up on any who try to stop us."

The Feld were obedient and moved quickly to follow the orders. Caleb rode next to Jeremiah in the front wagon, his TatTat at his feet within easy reach.

The wagons moved slowly through the crowd. The Feld tossed loaves of bread and big hunks of cheese to the starving masses. That enabled them to move forward. It also meant they now had a huge mob trailing the wagons and most were armed.

As they neared the Barco, other lights went on, both on the ground and on the roof. The blimp was directly overhead only 100 feet or more above the building. It was descending fast.

Jeremiah shouted as loud as he could, trying to be heard over the screams of the mob. "Now." Hands reached into the wagon. Guns and rockets came out instead of food. Several rockets soon launched toward the blimp. Two dove into the ground just a few hundred feet away, dropping like wounded ducks into deadly explosions.

Three others fired into the sky and missed the massive blimp. Jeremiah took careful aim. The Suisse-made rocket didn't disappoint. It fired straight and slammed into the blimp's gondola. It burst into a huge roar of flame and shrapnel.

The crowd screamed in anger as guards raised their guns to target the attackers. Feld guns lashed out with fury. Dozens of bullets tore into the crowd behind the wagon. Caleb raised the TatTat and aimed it at the guards, amazed at the lack of recoil. He tried to blot out that he was killing and focused on what had to be done.

Soon bullets were flying back at the Feld. Two men were already down and the others took cover around the wagon.

Then the others began to attack. An entire, well-armed company of Feld opened up on the mob from behind. The crowd began to drop by droves. The Englisch wailed in fear and ran, abandoning their guns and climbing over one another to escape the trap.

More fell and blood covered the broken concrete ground.

Caleb saw one of the mob aim a gun at Jeremiah. He dove in front of the deacon and held down the trigger of the TatTat. The woman fired, hitting Caleb in the left arm, just before her body was torn apart, as Caleb's burst caught her right in the chest. As she collapsed, blood flew from a half-dozen wounds. It was only then he realized that she had been the flesher who'd offered her body for a price.

The Feld company was soon unopposed and moved through the city capturing or killing the dean's men. Most were too drunk to fight back and surrendered with ease. It was equally easy to seize the factory as well. The equipment and guns were too valuable to destroy, so they prepared them for transport. The wagons would take back the food and then return to gather guns and equipment.

Jeremiah walked over to the wounded acolyte who sat on a concrete step crying. The deacon carried something under his coat, hiding it from Caleb.

"I killed her."

"You saved me. You had no choice. None of us did. But you did good. And good deeds are rewarded." He pulled the bobbeli from under his coat.

"Wha, what are you going to do with the buwe?" For a brief second, he feared the answer.

"I know a good mamm who will take care of him," he said, thinking of Hannah and her welcoming homestead. "And I doubt the Feld will mind if a few of these Suissie gold pieces go missing as well."

Caleb nodded as the tears began dry.

It had been a long, bloody night, and Jeremiah knew it would be his last. He'd served his time, and it was about time he found some peace, a well-earned retirement. Hannah was a handsome woman in need of a husband. Maybe it was time he went back to farming.

~END~

The Tesla Code
By Martin T. Ingham

"And Thus God struck him dead!" shouted the man in a wide-brimmed felt hat, a local Amish councilman.

The crowed stood quietly around the town square, gazing upon the body of a local watchmaker, Eli Phelps. The formerly healthy man of thirty years, a seemingly devout man with a wife and seven healthy children, was now a charred mess. The skin was blackened and blood trickled from his ears and nose, the result of heavenly retribution.

"This," the councilman continued, picking up a charred wooden box. "This was what drew the Lord's ire." He pried open the lid of the box to reveal a mess of copper wires. "This forbidden technology."

A few in the crowd gasped, but most remained silent, some nodding in agreement or understanding. It was a rare, yet not unheard of, occurrence. Those who dabbled in technology, who dared to summon the power of God known as "electricity" were struck dead by His own hand.

"It is one of the most high commandments, to fashion no idols above God. The almighty's judgment is swift and just." The councilman concluded by tossing the charred box on top of the dead man's body and walking away.

Two cloaked men emerged from the crowd and gathered up the body and box, and scurried after the councilman as obedient servants.

Daniel Veltman watched the crowd disperse from his uncle's storefront. He often loitered around with Uncle Roy during supply runs for his parents, but this day he had a good excuse to pause. The incident with the watchmaker had drawn everyone's attention, as it should have. What a tale he'd have to tell when he got back to the farm.

With the spectacle concluded, Daniel ventured back into his uncle's shop, to pick up the important leather goods his father had ordered.

The shop was well lit by tall windows during daylight hours, and several hanging chandeliers held oil lamps for darker times. A large, layout table sat in the middle of the large space, with racks of finished goods and raw materials lining the four walls of the modest shop. Belts, coats, saddles, boots; if it was made with leather, Uncle Roy would make it; an skilled leather craftsman of the Midwest.

"How was the show?" Uncle Roy asked as Daniel came over to the layout table. There, Roy sat over a half-finished set of riding chaps.

"Never seen anything like it before," Daniel replied, removing his straw hat and wiping his forehead. "Mr. Phelps' body, it, I mean, it…"

"Blackened and burned, like somebody set him on fire," Uncle Roy answered for his stuttering nephew.

"I heard the stories, sure. It's part of schooling, but seeing it in person," Daniel said, trailing off.

"I've seen it many times," Uncle Roy continued. "Men who get it in their heads to tinker with the old technology. Yes, the reckoning destroyed everything of the so-called decadent past, but there are still books and diagrams. Illegal, of course, deemed satanic by the High Ordnung Council, but still it exists."

"But why would anyone tempt the Lord like that?" Daniel asked. "Do they not believe they will die for it?"

"Some don't," Uncle Roy replied. "Others think they can avoid it, or that there's a secret to the power, some way to circumvent God's law. Then again, there are those who don't believe it is God, even now."

Daniel shook his head in disbelief. "I'd say that's pretty compelling proof."

"Is it?" Uncle Roy asked with a peculiar inflection.

"Uncle?" Daniel asked.

"Is it proof of God? Or is it something altogether different that we don't understand?"

"The ways of God are clear," Daniel replied, feeling his heart shake in his chest. What was his Uncle doing, hinting at heresy? Was it some kind of twisted test? Some in the family said that Uncle Roy possessed a dark sense of humor, though it wasn't something he'd ever shared with youngsters. Though, Daniel was nearly sixteen, virtually a man, so perhaps his uncle no longer considered him a child.

"Your faith is firm," Uncle Roy mentioned, returning his attention to his leather for a brief moment before continuing. "You well understand the law, as taught by the Ordnung and history. You know that mankind once sought to harness God's power, build machines to tap into divine energy, and that the Lord answered that disobedience with death from above."

"As he still does to this day," Daniel added. "Mr. Phelps was proof of that."

"Phelps was a fool," Uncle Roy said. "A cocky, arrogant fool."

"Must have been," Daniel remarked, having not known the man himself, yet his death at God's hand taught him much of the man's character, enough to justify his uncle's assertion.

Uncle Roy grunted, and turned back to his tools again. He grabbed a large needle and began weaving heavy twine into the leather. Several loops passed through the material and he said nothing more, proving he was done with the conversation.

"Did I say something wrong?" Daniel asked, as an awkward silence persisted.

"You did not know Eli Phelps, yet you cast judgment upon him. Just as everyone will because of the nature of his death."

"I was agreeing with you," Daniel defended. "You called him a fool."

"And I have that right, having known him for years. I was a guest at his house on many occasions, and so I understand the meaning of his foolishness where others, like yourself, will not."

"I'm sorry, I didn't know he was your friend."

"He will have been nobody's friend by the end of the day," Uncle Roy added. "Nobody will want to have their name associated with his. The sin he committed will condemn his wife and children to be shunned, outcasts. They'll starve, or worse, to set an example for those who would dare tempt fate—to scare those who might be willing to risk their lives to quench their curiosity. For it is one thing to condemn yourself, but it takes a special kind of fool to threaten his own family."

"Wise words," Daniel affirmed.

"Just common sense," Uncle Roy corrected, "and there lies the true sin. How is it right that man condemn a family for the actions of one man? If it were 'God's will," wouldn't He strike them down himself?"

Daniel was at a loss for words, and before he could formulate his answer, Uncle Roy continued.

"Belief is quite a double-edged sword. If you truly believe it is God that strikes dead those who tinker with old technology, then you must cede that God will punish all those who offend him. Otherwise, why would he only strike down those who play with wires and circuits, batteries and capacitors? Why would he need man to do his dirty work, when he clearly is doing a good job of it, himself?"

"I... can't answer that," Daniel finally uttered.

"And some would call that thought heresy," Uncle Roy said before glancing down at his handiwork which had been halted by the conversation yet again. "I fear I really must get these chaps done before nightfall. Your father's commission is sitting behind the counter at the front." With that, he returned his full attention to the leather.

Daniel nodded and turned to the counter, where he found a pair of heavy boots waiting. They were well made and very plain, devoid of any decorative features. Plain was Godly, and all things functional in the modern world.

It was the way of things, all that Daniel had ever known; a world ruled by the beliefs of the Amish.

*

Dinnertime was unusually quiet and solemn. Word of the incident in town had spread already, and it left an air of discomfort. It was never easy to lose members of the community, and the circumstances behind the deaths were scandalous, which made it ever worse.

Daniel wasn't feeling very hungry, as he picked at his mashed potatoes and corn, pondering the words of his uncle. The mixed messages he got weren't helping his state of mind.

Mother coughed, and then coughed again.

Everyone seemed to ignore it, but Daniel stared over attentively. It was nothing new, a worsening condition that had been plaguing her for years now. Prayers seemed to ease the suffering, though thus far the Lord had yet to cure poor Elizabeth Veltman. Doctor Heffler said it was an autoimmune disorder, her own body attacking itself, but there was little he could do.

The old legends began to trickle over Daniel's thoughts. Tales of miraculous medicines of the ancient times, before God had returned to remove the Devil's technology. It was said they had been able to cure most anything, but somehow that had not been God's will. Some said it in fact defiled God's creation, but prolonging life when the Lord had deemed it's time to be over. Others said it was all fables designed to tempt the weak willed into seeking forbidden knowledge.

Like most boys, Daniel had fantasized about the past, read a few underground books about the days of cities and skyscrapers, the kind of stories your father would whoop you for if he ever found out. But never had Daniel ever thought it was more than just a passing flight of fancy to think of it.

Yet now, he had to wonder. Could there have been something to those stories?

Clearly, there was something. Why else would God strike down those who dared to experiment? Why, indeed.

Mother pushed her barely-touched plate aside and excused herself, clearly in pain. Father got up and escorted her out, leaving the seven children to finish their meal. Daniel's oldest sisters were accustomed to handling clean-up. In the last year, they had taken over a majority of the household chores, as mother became less and less capable.

The silence spoke for the Veltman children. They were already mourning the loss of their mother, before she was even in the ground. Death was all but certain.

*

After dinner, as the plates were being washed by the younger children, Daniel found his father sitting in the living room by the fireplace, reading the Bible by lamplight. Daniel could see the worn old book opened to the book of Psalms, and knew his father was seeking comfort in the scriptures.

"Thank you for retrieving my new boots," Father said, looking up from the book.

"Of course," Daniel replied, his heart heavy with sadness.

"There is something on your mind that you wish to discuss?" Father asked after an awkward silence.

"I had a rather odd conversation with Uncle Roy this afternoon," Daniel said.

"I can imagine," Father said, glancing back down at the Bible. "My big brother has always been something of a heretic. Do not let it bother you."

"But it does, Father," Daniel replied, unable to mask his emotions.

Father gently shut the good book and rested his hands on his lap. "How so?"

"It is difficult to say," Daniel admitted. "It's making me question… things."

"Of course," Father said. "Doubt is always a danger, and ever-present condition of man. Much as Thomas, man requires proof of the Lord, yet we have it daily, in all his creation. And today's events should be further assurance that God's hand is very real. Trust your eyes, and fear not."

"It's my eyes that make me fear," Daniel rebutted. "I see great horror, death attributed to God, and I wonder why."

"It is not our place to question," Father rebuked. "Live your life simply, as we have for generations, and there will be no need to worry about the Lord's retribution on Earth, and your seat shall be assured at His table in Heaven."

It had all been said before, and Daniel hadn't expected anything more from his father. It was as it was, the devout speech and strong faith of a true believer. Growing up, it had been enough to hear, but now, life was no longer as simple.

"And what of mother?" Daniel asked.

Father lowered his head and in a rare sign of emotion tears formed in his eyes. "I'm afraid she will soon be with our Lord."

After an extended pause, Daniel continued. "I can't help but wonder, what if there was more we could do for her."

"We have done all that we can. She is in God's hands now."

"But the old legends tell of devices and medicines…"

"Lies," Father snapped. "Deceptions of the Devil, meant to lure those weak of faith to their doom."

"But what if there was something to them? What if a forbidden technology could save her? Wouldn't it be worth exploring?"

"Better to die by God's plan than to live on through Satan's machinations." Father stood up from his seat, clearly tired. "Give this no more thought."

Daniel watched his father leave the room, and then stared at the lingering embers in the fireplace. Ancient legends spoke of fire being a forbidden technology once upon a time. Perhaps there was more to life than blind obedience. Yet, some truth was plain to see. Anyone who dared tinker with the wrong science wound up dead, whether by God or something else.

How did one hide themselves from God?

*

The funeral was held on a sunny September afternoon. It was an all

146

too familiar affair for Daniel. It was every year that he lost someone he cared about. Today, it was his mother, last year, his little sister, the year before that his neighbor and youthful playmate Ezekiel Riley. Death was an all too common occurrence, but something that was part of life.

Yet, Daniel wondered how much a part of life it had to be.

Father threw a handful of dirt on the coffin as it was lowered into the ground, and Daniel turned to see his uncle holding back, leaning against a birch tree, his arms folded and a sorrowful scowl on his face. Daniel felt compelled to see how he was doing.

"A waste," Uncle Roy simply said.

"Father would say it's God's will."

"Perhaps. In part," Roy shot his eyes over to the coffin and then stared right at Daniel. "But that's also a sad excuse for our own ignorance."

"The doctors did all they could. There is only so much man can do."

"Today, perhaps," Roy darted his eyes back to the mourning crowd. "But centuries ago, perhaps not so much."

"What do you mean?" Daniel asked, confused by his uncle's strange demeanor.

"Come back to my shop," Roy said as the mourners began to disperse. "I could use a hand with something."

"Okay," Daniel replied, suspicious of his uncle. He had never seen him so distracted. The man had just lost his older sister, but that didn't really explain his squirrely behavior. There was something else going on, and Daniel needed to know what.

*

"What If I told you, there could have been a way to save your mother?" Uncle Roy asked as the shop door shut.

"We did everything we could," Daniel rebutted.

"Yes, everything we could do with our current limitations," Roy said, making his way over to a heavy desk in the corner. He reached down and rifled through a pile of leather until he retrieved a ratty stack of paper hiding underneath. He slapped them down on the desktop and motioned for Daniel to look.

The top sheet was torn and brown, discolored with age, and the gloom of the shop made it difficult to read. As a lamp flickered to life, Daniel's vision revealed the type on the cover, "*United States Department of Defense, Project 673321-C, Codename: Tesla.*"

"This is the true reason our technology is restrained," Roy explained. "It's a closely guarded secret. Even most of the Ordnung don't know about it."

Daniel began to leaf through the sheaf of papers, seeing diagrams and numerical equations he couldn't fathom. Much of what he saw went way over his head, and then he flipped back to the front and skimmed the summary, which explained the bare truth of it.

"You see, it's not God who strikes down anyone who plays with electricity," Roy said as Daniel read the project summary. "It's this Tesla project, a series of machines circling in the heavens that bring down death upon anyone who tries to utilize electricity."

"This is unbelievable," Daniel said. "But how... if this is true... how could anyone hide such a thing?"

"Rulers always have their reasons," Roy replied. "Some buried the truth in the name of maintaining order, others because they wanted power. These days, it's all because after centuries of perpetrating a lie they honestly don't know any better."

"And so they blame God," Daniel uttered, as the truth sank in.

"Yes," Roy said, grabbing the papers and returning them to their hiding place under the leather scraps. "So, you see, our technology is not restrained by the divine, but by men who are long dead. Before this Tesla Project, there were medical devices, scanners and medicines, that could cure most any ailment. People lived in huge buildings that towered over the Earth, and they traveled faster than any horse could run in decoratively painted metal carts. People even traveled beyond the sky, to the moon and stars. This is the truth that has been buried and silenced."

Daniel's sorrow after losing his mother was quickly fading, supplanted by a growing anger, for a great part of his life felt like a lie. Everything he knew, everything he had been taught, relied on the fear of a God that was evident in all things. Yet, not everything was God. So much of it was man!

Mixed with the anger was a sense of betrayal, for here he stood, with an uncle who had clearly known the truth all along but never told him. Daniel couldn't tell how much of it was because his uncle had waited this long to explain it, and how much was because he had told it at all.

"Why?" Daniel asked through gritted teeth. "Why tell me this now?"

Uncle Roy paused and looked around, as if wary of someone overhearing, despite their being alone in a locked building. "Because we're going to stop it."

"Wait, what? Who's we? And how are *we* going to stop anything?"

"The particulars will have to wait until we are underway. But I need to know, are you willing to commit yourself to the cause?"

"To ending this curse that holds us down? Of course!" Daniel answered emphatically.

"Good," his uncle said, looking quite happy. "A group of us will be heading west tomorrow, to undo what our ancestors did. It has been hundreds of years in the making, this journey."

"Then I'm coming with you," Daniel said.

Uncle Roy patted him on the shoulder and stood up. "Meet me here at dawn, and remember to pack light. Oh, and here—" Uncle Roy dug a silver round out of his pocket and handed it to Daniel.

"What is this?" Daniel asked, having never seen its like.

"It's a coin from the old Republic," Uncle Roy explained. "If we get separated, or you need help and I'm not around, this can open doors. Those who know the truth will recognize this, and know you're one of us."

The large coin was worn but still heavy, and the lettering was strange, hard to decipher. One side had the visage of a pretty woman, and the other a broad eagle. It was the sort of imagery forbidden by scripture, as such was deemed idolatry. The only money Daniel had ever seen was plain, with basic details and little artistry.

"This must be worth a fortune," Daniel remarked.

"It's priceless," Roy said. "Keep it safe, just in case. Now go on, get going. Best not keep the family waiting."

*

The packing was easy. The leaving was not.

After a quiet dinner, which was the norm now that mother had passed, Daniel threw a change of clothes and a few basic survival tools in a sack, preparing for the journey. He had no idea how long it would take or what might transpire along the way, though he was confident that it was a righteous mission.

Yet, he could not leave unannounced.

Father was never one for late hours, so it would have been a simple thing to slip out in the night, but that would not have been fair to the family. To leave them wondering would not only cause them undue worry, but could also draw attention to things that had to remain secret.

As his sister Anne was putting away the dishes, Daniel found father sitting by the fire, staring at the smoldering embers as the final log dwindled down to a slim streak of coals.

"Things are returning to normal," father remarked as Daniel sat down in an adjacent chair. It creaked slightly with age as it took his weight.

"I'm not sure normal is ever a thing," Daniel replied, pondering the meaning of the word. A day or two ago, it would have been a simple fact, but now, understanding how the world had been altered, he wondered how "normal" this life of theirs had ever been; truly a false existence forced upon them by past meddling. Though, wasn't that also the way of time? Everyone's state of being affected by the actions of previous generations, which created normalcy. Every action, or inaction, forges a path to the future, and each change created a new normal; a constant cycle of change and familiarity. Such was the paradox.

Father nodded his head, seeming to understand Daniel's meaning, at least in part.

"There is something I have to do," Daniel blurted out, finding no easy way to start. "Uncle Roy has a journey planned, and he's asked me to accompany him."

"Harvest begins in a few weeks," father said. "Truly bad timing. Your uncle can manage without you, but the farm would hurt by your absence."

"Jacob is old enough to oversee the reaping," Daniel rebutted, "and we always need a few hired hands, regardless."

"You had best give a very good reason for leaving your family to work in your absence," father said coldly.

What could he say? Dare he admit the truth of the matter? It seemed that secrecy was key, but how could he explain his departure in a way that his father could accept?

"There's a courtship involved," Daniel finally said.

"Oh?" Father's tone abruptly shifted, sounding more positive.

"It's a leather merchant's daughter, in the west. Uncle Roy has some connections, and he's invited me along."

"Well, that I can understand," father said, sounding more jovial than usual. "Though I was hoping you'd find a local girl. Though, I suppose we find love in mysterious places. I recall a story of my grandparents, who met on a stagecoach. They were both traveling to visit family, out west as a matter of fact."

"Then perhaps it is fate, this trip of mine," Daniel said.

"Indeed, though you will be missed."

It was both reassuring and disconcerting, to have lied to father. Though it would be a great disappointment when Daniel returned without a wife in tow, the true success of their mission would be ample compensation. And who knows what else he might find along the way?

*

The dim glow of the setting moon lingered in the sky as Daniel walked into town. There was a great commotion, far too much for the pre-dawn. Something was wrong.

Turning the corner to get a glimpse of his uncle's shop, Daniel's heart sank in his chest. The warden's armored wagon was clearly identifiable, waiting directly in front of the shop. This was no coincidence, and the authorities had no business being out at this early hour, unless there was a heretic to be arrested.

Flickering torches appeared, exiting the shop—four men, two holding the light, the others dragging Uncle Roy by the shoulders, as he twitched and thrashed, looking half-conscious in his struggles.

As the wardens dragged him to the back of their vehicle, Uncle Roy shouted, "The truth will set us free. Find it!"

Daniel knew in his heart that the message was for him. Somehow, he had to carry on with the mission, and break the system that had been enslaving all of humanity for centuries. Though, how he would do that eluded him. His uncle had been the one with the contacts and the knowledge. Daniel only knew the barest of truths, without the specifics that would be required to enact any kind of change.

As the warden's wagon thundered down the cobblestones of main street, Daniel ducked down a side alley and waited amidst empty barrels, paralyzed with fear and indecision. Minutes passed like hours, until he finally worked up the courage to venture forth.

Going back to his uncle's shop was not an option. If the wardens were out, they could be looking for accomplices. Though he'd done nothing wrong, obviously the council must think he had. Purely thinking the wrong way could get you in a lot of trouble sometimes, and the papers Uncle Roy had had—those were damning. Conspiracy to meddle with technology, or something to that effect. It was a serious crime, one of the few punishable by death.

A little voice in the back of Daniel's mind told him to forget it all, go back to the farm and live the life God had mapped out for him. Simply obey and enjoy the simple life—find some local girl who'd put up with him and give him as many children as she could bare... until God saw fit to take her, like mom.

Knowledge had the nasty habit of corrupting the innocent, or so many sermons said. Finally, Daniel understood what those preachers had meant. He couldn't forget what he knew and live life as he had. Now that he'd seen the truth, he had to do something about it.

There were others out there. Uncle Roy hadn't been planning this trip by himself. There were others out there who knew about the Tesla Project. It was just a matter of finding them.

Digging into his front pocket, Daniel retrieved the silver round his uncle had give him, *just in case*. This relic of a forgotten era was his key to finding the others who knew the truth.

The mission was on.

~The End... for now...

Also Available from Martinus Publishing

Bruno Lombardi's Snake Oil
A cynical "First Contact" adventure!

"A compelling exploration of what could happen if Earth's first alien visitors turn out to be a bit more like us, after all."

http://www.martinus.us/books.html#snakeoil
ISBN#978-0-6159936-6-9

Also Available from Martinus Publishing

Our Heroes Through Tomorrow
-by Dan Gainor

Six scintillating stories from a modern master of
speculative fiction!

~Available exclusively for the Kindle~
http://www.martinus.us/books.html#as02